## "If you let h[...]

Molly broke her stare and swallowed hard against the threat of tears.

"Molly." He said nothing but her name. But the way he said her name said everything. If she'd had any doubt of how strong the pull was growing between them—a pull she knew she had to ignore—the tone of his voice and his eyes confirmed it.

"This has to be about Zack. I have to be sure you know that." She wouldn't come out and say "It can't be about me," so she had to trust that her words got the message through. This would have been so much easier if there weren't volumes behind his eyes, if he didn't radiate that lost-but-noble-soul vibe that always did her in.

"Zack is the most important thing here," he said. While the solemnity of his tone put her a bit at ease, it also implied Zack's needs weren't the *only* thing here. Was Sawyer's telling choice of wording a skilled response or simple truth?

**Allie Pleiter**, an award-winning author and RITA® Award finalist, writes both fiction and nonfiction. Her passion for knitting shows up in many of her books and all over her life. Entirely too fond of French macarons and lemon meringue pie, Allie spends her days writing books and avoiding housework. Allie grew up in Connecticut, holds a BS in speech from Northwestern University and lives near Chicago, Illinois.

### Books by Allie Pleiter

### Love Inspired

#### *Wander Canyon*

*Their Wander Canyon Wish*
*Winning Back Her Heart*
*His Christmas Wish*
*A Mother's Strength*

#### *Matrimony Valley*

*His Surprise Son*
*Snowbound with the Best Man*
*Wander Canyon Courtship*

#### *Blue Thorn Ranch*

*The Texas Rancher's Return*
*Coming Home to Texas*
*The Texan's Second Chance*

Visit the Author Profile page at Harlequin.com for more titles.

# A Mother's Strength

## Allie Pleiter

### LOVE INSPIRED
INSPIRATIONAL ROMANCE

# LOVE INSPIRED®
## INSPIRATIONAL ROMANCE

Recycling programs
for this product may
not exist in your area.

ISBN-13: 978-1-335-75875-0

A Mother's Strength

Copyright © 2021 by Alyse Stanko Pleiter

This edition published by arrangement with Harlequin Books S.A.

For questions and comments about the quality of this book, please contact us
at CustomerService@Harlequin.com.

Love Inspired
22 Adelaide St. West, 40th Floor
Toronto, Ontario M5H 4E3, Canada
www.Harlequin.com

**Printed in U.S.A.**

I sought the Lord, and he heard me,
and delivered me from all my fears.
—*Psalm* 34:4

To first responders everywhere

# Chapter One

Molly Kane stared at the double-shot Americano coffee with one sugar sitting waiting on the counter.

Sawyer Bradshaw was late.

It was 9:32 a.m. and Sawyer was never late. A mid-April snowfall wasn't rare enough to make anyone late in this part of Colorado. No, her "right after 9:00" customer with the sad, gold-hued eyes was as constant as the sunrise.

Constancy aside, he'd become a favorite customer. He always thanked her profusely for the waiting coffee. It tugged at her heart the way he seemed so startled by her kindness.

Her request today would surely startle him. *You've got to make this work, Lord. Zack needs it.* The request she was about to make on behalf of her son was beyond brave to ask someone she'd never seen anywhere but here at The Depot. In fact, she only knew his name from the badge pinned to his work shirt.

Molly had spent half the night last night talking herself into believing that loner Sawyer had ended up in an "everybody knows everybody else and pokes their nose into everyone's business" town like Wander Canyon for a reason. Her reason—or rather, Zack's. Now, as she watched the minutes tick past, doubts made her stomach tumble.

Sawyer's truck pulled up just before 10:00 a.m., sending a pop of relief to fill her chest.

"Chilly day. I'll just warm this up for you, Sawyer," she said as he pushed through the door of the old train car repurposed into a unique coffee shop. Sawyer gave a weary grunt as he shook the damp spring snow off his shoulders.

He'd shown up every other morning at exactly 9:13, straight off his shift as the night watchman at Mountain Vista Golf Resort. Molly nodded toward the clock as she poured hot coffee into the already strong espresso drink. "Not like you to be late." That seemed a less invasive question than "Is everything okay?"

He rolled his shoulders. "Bit of a day. Bit of a night, actually."

"Well," she said, adding a deliberate cheer to her voice as she slid the steaming mug across the counter toward Sawyer. "Hope this helps. Because, well, I need to ask a favor. Kind of a big one, actually."

Sawyer stared in surprise at the stoneware mug. Every other morning, he took his coffee in a to-go cup. "Uh… Molly?"

He'd never used her name before. She took that as a good sign.

Molly flashed a quick look to Pastor Newton, who had been sitting in a nearby booth waiting for Sawyer as long as she had been. Pastor Newton thought her idea was a bit far-fetched, too, but he was at least willing to lend his support.

"I was kind of hoping you'd stay and drink this one. Got a minute?"

Sawyer's surprise turned to shock. "I...suppose." He looked suspicious—wary, even—as he slid the three one-dollar bills and a trio of silver quarters onto the counter. He paid with exact change every morning. Molly pictured sets of coins and bills lined up on his kitchen counter each week—it was the kind of thing Zack would do.

Her seven-year-old son waged his battles with anxiety through fastidious rituals just like that. Shoes lined up. Books in color order. The same breakfast at the same time on the same plate every morning. The similarities were what had given her the idea she was about to launch.

"Come on over and sit down, Sawyer," Pastor Newton said as Molly nodded to her coworker and untied the apron from around her waist. Sawyer hesitated, clearly wondering what was going on.

Pastor Newton smiled as if he asked total strangers to join him for coffee every day—because, in fact, he often did.

"Did you know Molly has a son? Zack's in the second grade. He's a special boy."

Molly tried not to cringe. Zack *was* special. Still, people too often used "special" to avoid using "odd" or "troubled."

Zack was also struggling. Badly. Only a mother's desperation would produce the bravery needed to make the request she had in mind. A wild solution for an enormous problem.

Molly avoided Sawyer's suspicious eyes as she brought her double-whip mocha latte to the table to join Sawyer and Pastor Newton.

Molly took a deep breath. It was never an easy thing to admit Zack's troubles. And now she was going to lay it all out to someone she only knew as one of her customers.

Molly had a gift for seeing hurt souls, for seeing the people who sulked through life like a shadow. Sawyer was one of those. She had to believe he'd understand.

"Zack is an anxious boy. Every once in a while, it gets the best of him." She paused, trying to gauge Sawyer's reaction to that statement.

"Why don't you tell Sawyer what you told me yesterday?" the reverend suggested.

"Lately he's been struggling much more." *Tell him all of it. He needs to hear all of it.* "Actually, the school nurse found him curled up in the utility closet at before-school care yesterday. It took her twenty minutes to talk him out."

"The counselor he's been seeing was helping, wasn't she?" Pastor Newton's voice was encouraging.

"Yes. Mrs. Hollings felt we were making progress. Some, at least. More good days than bad." Molly twisted the paper napkin she'd brought over between her fingers. It almost made her laugh—Zack twisted rubber bands between his fingers when he was nervous, and she was certainly nervous now. "It's been a while since we had something like this. No one can figure out what brought it on. Sometimes I think nothing at all brings it on. It just comes."

Molly ignored Sawyer's "Why are you telling me this?" expression and pressed on.

"Mrs. Hollings and I brought him to the nurse's office for a few minutes and got him ready for class. Eventually. Which is better than the last time where we just had to give up and go home."

"That's good," the pastor said. "Progress, right?"

"It doesn't feel like it." Molly wrapped her hands around the stoneware mug. "She had an idea. It might sound absurd, but at this point I'm willing to try anything."

Pastor Newton turned to Sawyer. "Jean Hollings is very good at her job. And very creative."

Molly leaned in toward Sawyer. She wasn't going to leave a single stone unturned to help Zack find the emotional footing that kept eluding him. Second grade had turned out to be a disastrous year, and if she didn't do something soon, it was going to take a monster of a battle to get Zack back into school in the fall. Into the third grade, even. She had to find a way to make the current year end on something close to a high note.

"That's sort of where you come in."

"Me?" Sawyer tried not to gulp. He barely knew Molly.

Sure, he was a near-daily customer, but he'd never told her how much he liked this place. He didn't make small talk. He hadn't even known she had a son, until this moment. How on earth did he get swept up in whatever it was Molly had in mind?

"Mrs. Hollings seems to think Zack needs an outlet." Molly took a deep breath and nervously braced herself against the table. "Something to build up his confidence, to feel as if he could be good at something. Something sort of physical, so he can burn off some of that nervous energy that keeps drowning him." Molly's eyes held a hopeful gleam that was near frantic.

"Doesn't the town have a Little League or something?" Sawyer said, stumped for any other response.

She gave a forced, tight laugh. "A team sport won't work. I'm talking more on the 'sort of' side than the 'physical' side."

"So I take it Jean had a suggestion." Pastor Newton urged her on.

Molly took another deep breath. She hadn't even touched the coffee she'd brought to the table; she just kept wringing that paper napkin within an inch of its life. "She did. Like I said, it's a bit weird, but honestly, there isn't anything I wouldn't try."

"Of course," the pastor said. "You're his mother."

Sawyer fought the feeling of being cornered. The whole point of him coming to Wander Canyon was to be invisible. To work out the kinks of the last year without anyone watching. To *not* get involved. His one indulgence had been his morning trips to The Depot for coffee. And now, from the looks of it, that indulgence was about to get him into a whole lot of…of what? Trouble? Involvement? Small-town drama?

Molly looked at him with pleading eyes. "Mrs. Hollings seems to think Zack should try…golf."

Sawyer was sure he hadn't heard right. "Golf?" Even the pastor looked as if he was working to not look like he found the idea ridiculous. And weren't pastors supposed to play a lot of golf? Or was that just doctors?

Molly held up a hand and began to tick off a list of reasons Sawyer wasn't certain he wanted to hear. "It's not overly physical, but involves time out in open spaces. It's something he can do in a small way on his own and then bring other people into it when he's ready. It's—"

"One of the most frustrating sports on the planet," Sawyer butted in to stop her right there. "I could show you piles of golf clubs bent from their owners whacking them against a tree in frustration." He sat back, stunned. "Golf? Really?"

His astonishment clearly pushed her buttons. "Well, you don't have to put it quite that way. It's unusual, I know. But the more I think about it…it makes a kind of sense."

"It's an unusual solution for an unusual boy," Pastor Newton said. "Good for Jean for thinking out of the box. But I do wonder about one thing. Golf's not especially popular in this town. No offense, Sawyer."

"None taken," Sawyer said. "Just a job." Sawyer hadn't been blind to the smug reactions to his Mountain Vista name tag and uniform shirt. Folks in Wander Canyon harbored no good wishes for the resort. He'd heard the stories of how Mountain Vista had tried more than once to expand by making paltry offers for the land of struggling ranchers. Working for the bad guys suited him—people steered clear of him, and he liked that just fine.

"But you must play," Molly insisted. "You must know

how. I mean, nobody takes a job at a golf resort and doesn't golf, right?"

Oh, he didn't like where this was heading. "I'm bad at it."

Molly smiled. "That's great!"

Why on earth did that make her happy?

"That's exactly what Zack needs."

"Huh?"

"Someone who can help him see it's okay that he's not great at it. Someone to show him how, just enough so he doesn't feel any pressure about it."

The full realization of this woman's request hit him like a gust of wind. "You…you're asking me to teach your son to play golf?"

Molly straightened in her chair like that wasn't the most bizarre thing Sawyer had heard this week. Maybe this year. And it had been one whopper of a year. "Well, yes."

"Me?"

"I don't know anyone else who works at Mountain Vista, so, yes. What I *don't* need is someone from the long list of Wander folks who hate the place."

"She's right," Pastor Newton agreed. "Golf and Wander don't exactly get along these days."

Sawyer sat back in his chair, scrambling for excuses. Only a bafflingly short list came to mind. "It isn't even warm outside yet. I'm no golf pro. I hardly qualify as a duffer."

"What's that?" she asked.

"Someone who wishes he was a lot better at golf," Pastor Newton joked. "Or so I'm told. Lots of pastors golf. Just not around here."

"Zack doesn't need a golf pro." Was she doing that on purpose? Looking at him with wide, persuasive blue eyes that could melt the spring snow outside? "What Zack needs is a friend. Who plays golf, and kinda badly at that."

Sawyer swallowed hard and told himself it was perfectly reasonable to say no. He wished she hadn't leaned in and made her voice all soft and musical. "He needs someone who understands what it's like to be alone." She paused and took one final, heart-melting breath before adding, "I think that's you."

"He's a special boy," Pastor Newton repeated. "You could be doing him an amazing service. And Molly's right—there isn't anyone else in our little town in the position you are to do it."

Sawyer couldn't believe he was even thinking about it. Then that confounded woman pulled out the final piece of persuasion she knew he couldn't refuse. "Free coffee for a year."

Sawyer didn't reply. He was currently applying every ounce of his willpower to do the sensible thing and say no.

"I can't help thinking you were drawn to this place and Molly's coffee for a reason," the pastor said. "Things like this never line up by accident. You could change a little boy's life."

"You could *save* my little boy's life." Her face flushed a bit at the drastic words. "A bit dramatic, perhaps, but if things don't turn around for Zack soon... No seven-year-old should be this unhappy."

Now she was tearing up. Granted, Sawyer was well acquainted with looking like the bad guy, but refusing now would make him look like an ugly troll. Even so, Sawyer bit back the "Maybe" trying to leap recklessly off his tongue.

"All he needs is one small win, a foothold against the avalanche of 'not enough' that's plowing over his life. Please."

The word burrowed under the ten-foot-high wall Sawyer had built around himself and smacked into the one tender spot he had left. She looked tired, frustrated, helpless and beyond worried.

*"Please."*

"This idea makes no sense," Sawyer said, trying one last time to keep from giving in to her.

"Those are my favorite kind," she replied, brightening like a sunrise.

Sawyer found himself nodding, absolutely certain he'd regret it. Well, he was regretting a truckload of things lately, why not add this to the list?

# Chapter Two

Zack fidgeted in his chair, turning a blue rubber band over and over between his fingers as they sat in Cuccio's Pizza a few days later. Molly watched his dark brows—entirely too much like his father Steve's—furrow. "What if he's mean?"

"He's not mean. I know him from the coffee shop. He's actually very nice." "Very nice" might have been a bit of an overstatement, but Molly knew she was fighting an uphill battle here.

"What if I stink at it?"

She'd endured an endless stream of anxious questions from Zack since she'd set this date for him to meet Sawyer over pizza. That was just who Zack was, how he processed the world, but it taxed her extroverted patience no matter how much she loved her son. "We played mini-golf on vacation last year. You didn't stink at that." She tried to lean in playfully. "Besides, Mr. Sawyer says he's not very good at golf, either. You can stink at it together."

Zack's face told Molly he did not find that comforting. He began stretching the rubber band this way and that. "What if I hate it?"

It had been wise to get here fifteen minutes early. Not only because Zack always worried about getting to places on time but because it gave them a window to get all of these questions out of the way.

"If you hate it, you can stop. But you won't know if you hate it unless you try it. You might love it. You loved garlic bread and you were sure you were going to hate that, remember?"

Her son was unconvinced. "But you were sure I was going to love cream cheese and I hated that, remember?"

Oh, she remembered. *Cream cheese. Friendly, unassuming cream cheese. Who could hate that?* "Well, Mr. Sawyer strikes me as much more of a garlic bread kind of guy than a cream cheese one." As completely absurd as the description was, it rather fit the man. *Please, Lord*, she prayed as she looked toward the door. *Please let this go well. I need a way to help Zack, You know that.*

At precisely five o'clock, Sawyer walked in the door. She realized, with a shock, that this was the first time she'd seen him in anything other than his work clothes. He wore a long-sleeved T-shirt in a dark green, over dark blue jeans and boots that had seen better days. He was fit—lean and long in a way the work khakis and button-down shirt hadn't revealed. Were it not for the continually sad face and downcast eyes, he might have even been considered an attractive man. But his dark spirit, and the nonstop shadow that seemed to follow him wherever he went, outweighed any of his handsome features.

He scanned the small pizza shop for a second, more assessing the space than picking her and Zack out among the handful of customers. Steve's dad used to have the same reflex from his military days. It was more out of tactical habit for her former father-in-law than any fear, but Molly couldn't help but catch the caution in Sawyer's eyes.

"Zack, switch seats to this one," she said, patting the seat next to her so that it left the seat facing the door open for Sawyer. Her father-in-law had always needed to be seated facing the exit in any public space, so maybe Sawyer was the same. It made Molly realize she knew next to nothing about Sawyer's background. Still, her instincts and her prayers told her she could trust him with Zack—and those had never led her wrong yet. Well, except for Steve, but that was a whole other can of worms.

"Hi," she said cheerfully. "Thanks for coming. Best pizza in town. Also, the only pizza in town, so it's an easy win," Molly joked.

That almost brought a smile to the man's face. "Town joke?"

"I suppose you could say that."

Zack's eyes hadn't risen from his hands still fiddling with the rubber band. "Zack, this is Mr. Bradshaw. Can you say hello?"

Begrudgingly, Zack ventured a quick look at Sawyer and mumbled, "Hi."

Sawyer sat down. "Hi, there, Zack."

Molly waited a hopeful moment for Zack to offer

some other conversation. When he didn't, she turned with a bright smile to Sawyer and said, "What do you like on your pizza?"

To her surprise, Sawyer looked at Zack and said, "What do you like on yours?"

"Cheese," Zack said flatly. "Just cheese."

"I'm okay with just cheese," Sawyer said.

"Zack usually gets a mini cheese just for himself," Molly replied. "Have you ever had Hawaiian pizza? It's my favorite and they do a great one here." While Molly tried never to judge people, she did divide the world into those who "got" Hawaiian pizza, and those who found it a crime against nature.

"What's on a Hawaiian pizza?" Sawyer looked skeptical.

"Ham and pineapple mostly. But the other usual stuff, too."

"It's gross," Zack offered. Molly didn't know whether to be thankful for the conversation or annoyed at the critique.

"It sounds…unusual." It was clear Sawyer was trying not to say he found the concept *weird*. She'd heard that before. "I've never had it."

Here was a good place to demonstrate that other people tried things they didn't know if they would like. "If it's not your thing, I'll spring for another version." She hoped the "work with me" look she sent him hit home.

Sawyer's pause was long enough for Molly to worry that Zack was about to get another view of someone refusing to try new things.

"What if we just get one cheese and one Hawaiian?

That way Zack and I can share if it's not my thing. And if it is, then Zack will just have more pizza for himself."

Molly's heart just about skipped a beat when Sawyer looked at her son and said, "Okay by you?"

So few people ever really noticed Zack. She knew he liked it that way, that he preferred to blend into the woodwork and be unseen. Still, she yearned for him to have the courage to be in the world, to see all the wonderful things and people. To see the world as a marvelous place to be explored instead of a collection of bad things waiting to happen. Of course, she knew she was reading too much into a simple pizza dinner and a round of not-really golf lessons. *I'm desperate for a foothold, Lord. Even a tiny one. Could this please be it?*

The server came by and took their order. Sawyer winced when Molly announced this would be her guest's first taste of Hawaiian pizza.

"Some people think it's strange, but I like it," the young girl commented as she set down large plastic cups of their chosen soft drinks. Molly recognized the girl from one of the ranching families in town.

"Could you bring me an empty one of these?" Sawyer asked the server.

The young woman gave him a quizzical look before eventually replying, "Uh…okay." While she fetched the cup, Molly tried to remember if it was one of the ranches that had been targeted by Mountain Vista, but she couldn't. Sawyer had to know about the friction between the resort and the town, didn't he? Surely that was one of the reasons he always seemed to be hiding from view, much like Zack?

"Do you know anything about golf?" Sawyer asked Zack when the empty plastic cup arrived.

"Not really."

"We watched some on TV the other day," Molly added. She didn't find watching the sport the least bit interesting, but she pretended to for Zack's sake. She sat with her computer tablet beside Zack on the couch, looking up golfing facts and questions while they watched. "And we've been to a mini-golf course in Boulder."

To Molly's surprise, Sawyer reached into his pocket and produced a golf ball. "How's your aim?"

The question startled Zack enough to look up from his rubber band. "Huh?"

"Could you roll this across the table so that it fell into the cup on my side?"

Zack's eyes grew wide. "Here?"

Sawyer handed him the ball. "Right across the table. See the line in your mind between where the ball is and where it needs to go. Then roll it."

Zack looked at Molly as if he'd been asked to stand up on the table and sing "Happy Birthday" at the top of his voice. She could almost hear his thoughts, the cry of *Everyone will look at me and something bad will happen* that seemed to trail him every moment.

"Would it help if I did it first?" Sawyer asked.

When Zack nodded, Sawyer switched objects with Zack so that Zack held the cup and Sawyer held the golf ball.

"Okay, hold the cup against the table but tilted toward me. Keep it steady."

Zack hesitated, looked around the room, then complied. Sawyer glanced at the cup and then back at the ball in his hands, adjusted its position once or twice then rolled it across the round table so it fell into the cup with a crisp *plunk*. Zack immediately glanced around, sure all the other customers would notice this wildly un-restaurant-like behavior.

No one paid the least bit of notice.

"You try," Sawyer said, holding his hand out for the cup.

Cautiously, Zack watched Sawyer position the cup across the table. He set the ball down, then grabbed it up again. "What if I miss?"

"I catch it with this hand," Sawyer said, waving his other hand.

"What if someone sees?"

Molly envisioned a whole cascade of Zack questions about to spew forth, but Sawyer seemed undaunted. "They'll want their own ball, I expect."

"Who wouldn't want to play pizza golf?" Molly said with perhaps a bit too much enthusiasm.

It seemed forever until Zack lifted up the ball again, took a deep breath and rolled it across the table.

The plink of it hitting the bottom of the cup was the sound of victory.

There were a dozen more holes of "pizza golf"— including even one where they let her try—before their pizzas came. And when she missed and sent the ball bouncing onto the restaurant floor, Zack actually laughed instead of cringing.

Best of all, when Sawyer took his first huge bite of Hawaiian pizza, he actually smiled. "What do you know?" he said with genuine surprise. "It's actually good."

Zack rolled his eyes, but Molly felt the glow of a foot-hold take root. "So what do you think, Zack? Are you ready for your first golf lesson Tuesday?"

"Second," Sawyer corrected. "You just had your first."

Zack's eyes popped. "That wasn't a golf lesson."

"Sure it was. You sent a golf ball into a hole. That's golf."

"No, it's not." Molly was delighted to find Zack's tone more playful than challenging.

Sawyer, to her surprise, was playing right back. "Well, you didn't use a club, no, but the idea is the same. I have a weird way of teaching golf."

Weird or not, Molly thought this might actually work.


He should just keep walking.

Sawyer stood across the street from Wander Canyon Community Church on Sunday, a bag of pitiful bachelor groceries in his hand. His feet pointed in the direction where he should be going—home—but they wouldn't move.

While a couple of days this week had brought touches of snow, today was pure spectacular Colorado April. The days were still on the short side and could flip from warm to cold in a heartbeat, but the sun could shine like nobody's business. A bright, crisp day like today made him regret having to sleep through most of it, even if it was his day off.

The glory of the weather had drawn him outside,

walking the three blocks into town to stock up on canned soup and frozen dinners.

Frozen dinners that would thaw if he didn't get himself back home, but the sound coming out of the open church doors across the street from him glued him to the spot.

Church hymns—words like *love* and *spirit* and *Jesus*—floated out across the morning air. What the harmonies lacked in voices, they made up for in enthusiasm. He could pick out a strong bass, an unsteady tenor, a few hearty altos, and a soprano who clearly thought she could sing higher than she actually could.

And Molly.

There had to be at least a dozen voices coming from the church, but Molly's voice rang out sweet and clear above all the others. He'd heard her humming or singing softly at The Depot, but this was different. This was Molly singing full out, that bright spirit of hers shining through. He could easily picture her face. She'd have wide eyes and a smile as she sang. Her head would bob a bit to the rhythm, and one hand would float up with the notes as if she could push them toward the sky.

Some people had musical abilities. Others had musical gifts—talent and purpose that went far beyond notes or rhythms. Sawyer did his best to ignore what the sound of a piano did to his insides—more pain than joy. Music felt a world away from the man he was now.

Molly didn't just sing; she sent her heart out into the air. The choir could have been a hundred voices strong—instead of the struggling dozen Molly had told him it was—and still he'd have been able to pick out her voice.

What was a soggy Salisbury steak in the light of stealing moments inside that kind of joy?

"God love 'em, they try, don't they?"

Sawyer hadn't noticed that a man holding a whining toddler had walked up beside him.

"I give them credit," the man went on. "They don't have much to work with, but they sing their hearts out every Sunday. My wife included."

"She in there?" Sawyer nodded toward the church steps and the wide-open door.

"And right now we're not. A fact everyone is thankful for. Henry here has got a set of lungs on him, but he hasn't quite caught on to using them for singing. And I never did. Yvonne's not a great talent, but she loves adding her voice."

The man held out his free hand. "Chaz Walker. This is Henry." The toddler gave a grumpy sniffle and buried his head again in his father's shoulder.

Sawyer felt the familiar pull of reluctance to give his name. He avoided it at all costs anywhere near Denver, but thought it safe to say it here. "Sawyer."

"Pleased to meet you, Sawyer. I think I've seen you around town for a bit, but can't say we've met before now." The man was tall, with dark hair and features. The boots and stance led Sawyer to think he was from one of the ranches that still circled the small town. While the townspeople held little love for Mountain Vista, Sawyer knew the ranchers held no love at all.

"I don't get out much," Sawyer replied. "Night shift." Thankfully, enough people in town worked at the local medical center that people never immediately associated his night hours with the golf resort.

"And miss days like this?" Chaz said, looking up at the glorious sun just starting to touch the peaks of the nearby mountains. "I couldn't do it."

"I like the solitude," Sawyer offered, although *like* was perhaps too strong a word. He required it. It was a necessity rather than a preference.

"They let you inside, you know," Chaz hinted. Sawyer should have known the guy might have found a way to bring the conversation around to an invitation to church. Church people were like that—always wanting to bring you into the fold whether you were ready or not. Would Chaz be so eager if he knew who Sawyer was? The reason he was trying to stay invisible here in Wander Canyon? Not likely.

"Not my thing. I just stopped to listen for a bit." When that sounded a bit stalker-creepy, he added, "I've met Molly at The Depot and I recognized her voice."

"Molly Kane. Yeah, she's got a set of pipes on her. I think half the choir shows up on account of her. Either to hear her or because she twisted their arm to join." The man offered a small smile. "Watch out, you could be next."

"She's pulled a giant favor out of me already."

Chaz stared at him, connecting the dots. Had Molly told people what he was doing? Already? "Sawyer. Hey, you're the golf teacher, aren't you? The guy she's got helping Zack."

Sawyer didn't know quite what to say. "Teacher's an overstatement. I agreed to try out her wild idea. She said she needed a bad golfer, and I qualify." It made his skin itch that Molly had been telling people about him. His invisibility would likely slip away if she kept that up.

Chaz laughed and shook his head. "Yep, that sounds like our Molly. Wild ideas and pulling everybody into them."

Sawyer shifted the grocery bag. "I should get these home."

The voices across the street hit a boisterous crescendo and finished off the piece. Applause and shouts of "Amen!" wafted out the door.

"You could just come in for coffee. The stuff we serve doesn't quite match The Depot's, but the company's friendly."

"Oh, no," Sawyer answered quickly. He needed to get out of there before Molly caught sight of him. She'd absolutely drag him inside and introduce him around. "Hope you're able to keep the little guy happy," he offered, just because it seemed like the nice thing to say. After all, you could stand out by being too rude just as easily as you could stand out for being nice. Sawyer wanted to make sure he didn't stand out at all.

People were starting to come out the church door. "I gotta get this stuff home to the freezer before it melts." Sawyer turned to go and started moving as quickly as he dared.

"Good to meet you, Sawyer. Hope the golf thing works out," Chaz called.

"Thanks," Sawyer said, waving a hand rather than turning around. The last thing he wanted was for Molly to catch sight of him hanging around near the church and talking to people. She'd jump on that and he'd never hear the end of it.

Sawyer sat in his drab little kitchen that evening and stared at the black circle marking the date on the calendar page. The notation wasn't really necessary. He'd been counting down to the day for a year—it wasn't as if he could possibly miss its arrival.

April 17. One year since his life fell apart. It was stunning, really. In the space of sixteen city blocks, with a decision made in the blink of an eye, Sawyer had sent a law enforcement career down the drain.

He had made a single bad judgment. He'd let his view of his skills overshadow a more cautious choice. If Molly was looking for someone who knew how to fail, she'd found him.

There was no point in trying to stop his mind from reliving that fateful night. And his terrible mistake.

It wasn't just a terrible choice, it was a tragic one. A deadly one. High-speed pursuits—even involving the worst of criminals—were a huge risk in the city. He'd known that. And what had he done? He'd gone after Marcus Granger anyway. He had cursed that decision every waking moment since that night.

Granger had made a wild turn, lost control of his car and sent it hurtling toward Sawyer's squad car. Sawyer's desperate swerve to avoid a head-on collision had sent his own vehicle careening into the opposite lane. Right into the path of a minivan. Trying to avoid him, the driver had plowed the van into the corner of a brick building.

A whole family had died. A mom and two little boys who weren't doing anything but trying to get home.

The what-ifs circled him like moths. What if Marcus had spun out of control thirty feet later? What if Sawyer had caught up to him faster? What if he'd chosen not to pursue at all, and instead called for extra backup or air support, or picked any of the hundreds of other options open to him that night?

*You wouldn't be here. A walking mountain of regret who plods through a frosty golf course in the middle of the night in the middle of nowhere.* Even the joy in Molly's voice, still ringing in his mind, wasn't enough to drown out that kind of dark roar.

# Chapter Three

Tuesday afternoon arrived, bringing Zack's first lesson at the golf course. As Molly dropped her son off at the resort, Sawyer could see a mixture of excitement and worry warring on her features. There was a compelling, unnerving kind of beauty in how deeply she cared.

Sawyer wondered if he should admit that the same was going on inside his own chest. *I have no idea what I'm doing. And I can't mess this up.*

Fortunately, Zack gave Sawyer little chance to mull over his thoughts. Instead, the boy churned through a dozen worried questions before they even made it up the walk to the pro shop. Sawyer began to wonder if he'd just signed up for the longest hour of his life.

Zack stared at Sawyer's bag of clubs. Some of them practically came up to the boy's chest. The kid seemed small for his age and Sawyer knew he was a tall man. Zack eyed the clubs, which must have seemed massive, with dismay. "There's no way I can hold those."

Sawyer picked up his bag and shifted it to his other shoulder, away from Zack. "Of course not. These are yours." He pointed to another set of clubs leaning against the pro shop wall. "Most of them aren't much different than the ones you used at the mini-golf course. I guessed your height, but I think I got it right."

In a fit of surprise initiative, Sawyer had contacted the resort's pro shop to see if there was a children's set he could borrow. If Zack took to the game, Molly would need to buy him his own set, but that was a problem for another day.

Zack stared in wonder at the pint-size four-club set. It'd be weeks before the kid used anything but the iron or maybe the putter, but Sawyer figured Zack would want the consistency of having the same set each time. Plus, half the fun of golf was the gear, even if the thing looked like his own large golf bag had sprouted off a tiny newborn version.

Sawyer ignored the little tug he felt as Zack hoisted the small bag over his right shoulder exactly as he had. There was even a smile or two from a foursome of grandmother types getting into their cart to head to the first tee. Sawyer couldn't quite work out how the kid managed to look so cute and so terrified at the same time.

"Are we gonna play in front of all those people?" Zack gulped as they walked through the line of golfers loading bags into carts. He'd tried to pick a time when the course wasn't crowded, but it seemed any other people was too much of a crowd for Zack.

"No," Sawyer replied, glad he'd opted for this session to be on a small patch of green behind one of the maintenance sheds. Quiet and out of sight, Sawyer could feel Zack's tension ease as he realized they'd be hidden away here.

Things sort of went downhill from there.

Thirty minutes later, Sawyer found himself grasping for ways to keep Zack's anxious frustration under any kind of control.

"It won't go!" the boy shouted as his plastic Wiffle golf ball veered away from a wide circle Sawyer had spray-painted into the grass. "I can't get it to go."

The difference between the hand rolling "pizza golf" and the complexities of holding and aiming a golf club confounded Zack faster than Sawyer would have ever thought possible. The more wound up the kid became, the less he seemed able to master his hands to get any kind of control.

*Why did I ever think this would work?* After all, if anyone could teach anyone to play golf, why did courses invest in legions of pros? What had ever made him think this was a good idea?

Not what. *Who.* Molly needed this. He couldn't stomach the thought of letting her down.

"Okay," Sawyer said. "How about we stop for a moment."

Zack's child-size growl both struck a nerve and a funny bone in Sawyer. He certainly knew what it felt like to slam up against a brick wall no one else could see. As if the one thing he couldn't get right blocked anything else from ever being right.

Taking the club from the boy's hand, Sawyer sat down on the curb beside the small patch of grass. He laid the club down on the grass behind him and waited.

After pacing around a bit, Zack sank down beside him, a tiny ball of frustrated gloom. "It's no fun if I can't be good at it," the boy murmured.

"Did you think you'd be good at it today?" Sawyer asked carefully. He'd known golfers who had been at it for decades and still were unhappy with how they played. He was one of them, for that matter—a thought that grew new doubts as to the point of this venture.

"I thought it wouldn't be so hard," Zack admitted, scuffing his sneaker on the pavement.

"Hard or new?" Sawyer wasn't quite sure where the wisdom of that question came from.

Zack looked up at him. "What's the difference?" It wasn't a real question. More of a moan of resignation.

"New stuff always feels…lousy at first. At least for me." He thought about Molly's nonstop joy, and how foreign she'd find such a statement. She leaped through life like it was all some grand adventure.

And maybe that was half the trouble right there. "For people like your mom, maybe not so much. Seems to me she loves new things."

Zack's "tell me about it" frown told Sawyer he'd struck a nerve. "But for people like you and me," Sawyer went on, "new isn't much fun."

Zack looked up at him, a bit stunned. Lots of adults had probably given the kid endless speeches on courage and persistence and optimism and whatnot. Zack looked as if no one had ever admitted to him that life felt lousy sometimes. Then again, with a mom like Molly, that wasn't so hard to believe. While he found Molly's sunny optimism alluring, being around it all the time could likely be exhausting.

Sawyer went out on a limb. "So you can stop here, if that's what you want. But you got this set of clubs to use, and you know how to hold them now, too." Zack had, in fact, taken rather easily to adopting the correct grip of his club, even if the swing had eluded him. "Nothing wrong with saying that's enough for today. Now you got two things that won't be new next time, and then maybe the swing part will come to you."

"Or not," Zack added with a grumpy pout.

"Or not," Sawyer agreed. "Either's okay by me. But I kinda think maybe it's worth another try." When the boy looked unsteady, he added, "Back here, where nobody sees or cares how bad we are."

Using the word *we* lit some unwanted little glow in Sawyer's chest that he tried to ignore.

Zack seemed to consider this for a moment. "Mom'll be mad if I quit."

While the same thought had crossed Sawyer's mind, it wasn't exactly true. "Disappointed, maybe. Not mad. She just thinks this would be fun for you, and she wants you to have fun. Kids should have fun." That same weird, glowing tug made him add, "Fun seems kinda hard for you. Me, too."

Hard? Fun felt like it was off the table for the duration of his life. Now it was mostly marking time until everything didn't feel so awful. For the son of a cop, the nephew of a cop and the grandson of a cop, to be suspended from the force in shame was like cutting off an arm or axing his branch off the family tree.

He'd earned a lifetime of feeling that way for himself, but it seemed wrong for someone Zack's age to view life as something awful to be endured. Especially with a nonstop happy mom like Molly around. A useful impulse hit him. "Thirsty?" he asked. "We've got enough time to stop by the clubhouse and get something to drink."

"What if they don't have orange soda?"

Sawyer noticed the boy had ordered that with his pizza. "I happen to know that they do. Want some?"

Zack shrugged. "Okay."

It was a better ending to the day than frustration and sour faces. "They make good root beer, too."

"I saw you drink that at Cuccio's. Ick," Zack proclaimed.

"Don't like it, huh? Yeah, well, it's an acquired taste."

"I don't need to try it to know I'll hate it. It's all fuzzy."

"The foam? Oh, no, that's the best part. On a good day you get some on your nose and need to lick it off." Where was this chummy, friendly version of himself coming from? Joking about soft drinks with a second grader? Giving pep talks about golf? Being around Zack was bringing out a strange side of him.

Strange, yes, but not entirely unpleasant. It felt rather good, if he was honest with himself. As if even this failure of a golf lesson might be just the sort of okay-to-stink-at-it experience Molly seemed to think Zack needed.

As he and Zack sat at the outdoor picnic tables waiting for Molly to arrive, they shared their plastic cups of soda. Sawyer caught Zack trying not to stare at the generous dousing of foam that still topped the last bit of his root beer. "I'm telling you," he said, alarmed to find that his voice sounded almost teasing, "foam beats plain old bubbles any day."

"Does not." Pouty words, but the boy's face held just the smallest hint of a smile.

"Does, too. Not that you'd know, seeing how you've never tried it." Sawyer held up the glass. "Last chance."

There was just the tiniest hesitation before Zack shook his head.

"Okay, then." Sawyer drained his glass, making a big show of smacking his lips with enjoyment.

"You didn't get any on your nose," Zack pointed out.

"Things don't always work out the way you plan." Sawyer took the golf ball they'd been using from his pocket and rolled it across the picnic table toward Zack. He tilted his empty cup against the side of the table the way they had done in Cuccio's. "Sink it."

"I'll miss."

Sawyer raised an eyebrow. "You know that? For sure? 'Cause I don't."

He could read Zack's features so easily—the worried brow, the darting eyes, the fidgeting fingers. Something told him to wait the boy out, to give him this chance to decide on his own without nudges or encouragement.

Just as Molly's car was pulling up, Zack rolled the golf ball across the table to sink with a soggy but victorious plunk.

"Hole in one," Sawyer declared, almost embarrassed by the smile he felt stealing across his face.

"That's not a hole in one," Zack refuted.

"Trust me. On a lousy day, that's a hole in one. Besides, it doesn't feel so lousy now after all, does it? See what I mean about once things aren't new?"

Molly waved enthusiastically from her car window. The desperate sort of optimism in her eyes did things to the space under his ribs. He didn't know what to do with all the faith she was putting in him. She would indeed be heartsick if this—whatever this was—didn't help Zack. The knowledge sprung an odd surge of...of what? With a start Sawyer realized it was determination. Weird, new and definitely uncomfortable.

But not at all bad.

Molly counted the minutes until Sawyer walked in the door of The Depot the next morning. It had taken superhuman effort not to call the man last night when they got home from the grocery store after the golf lesson.

Most times she tried to do grocery shopping without Zack. The myriad of choices seemed to wind him up, and he was so particular about things that even the smallest adjustments—having to get a different kind of ketchup, for example—could send him into one of his tailspins.

It hadn't been nearly as bad this time. He kept mumbling something about "new" or she thought she heard him say "lousy" a couple of times, but Zack would refuse to explain himself when she asked.

The final aisle, the one where they kept the soft drinks, had been the showstopper. It had taken all her strength not to gasp in astonishment when Zack had made his surprise request.

"Root beer?!" she nearly shouted at Sawyer the moment he came through the door.

While a smile didn't reach his whole face—it never did—a bit of brightness sparked in his eyes. It sent her pulse jumping in ways that had nothing to do with a mother's gratitude.

Molly slid the ready coffee toward him, placing a

cookie on a napkin right beside it. "The cookie's also on the house if you can tell me how it is that you convinced my son he might want to try root beer? A *new* drink?"

Sawyer took the cup with just the tiniest hint of victory. "He did that?"

"So you didn't feel the world tilt last night? Because I did, in Becker's grocery store."

"We talked about the virtues of root beer, that's all. He told me he didn't like it. He also told me he'd never tried it."

Molly nodded. "Oh, I've had that conversation before. About a thousand times. *Usually* without any success."

"Did he like it?"

Molly let her grin drop. "No. Actually, he said it was 'lousy.'"

"Oh."

When Sawyer looked disappointed, Molly added, "But that's hardly the point. He tried it. He *tried* it. Do you have any idea how huge that is?"

"I'm guessing it's a big deal." He took a bite of the cookie—macadamia nut chocolate chip—and nodded his approval. She'd hidden the last one under the counter just so he'd get what she considered the best cookie The Depot served.

"How did you do it?" She really wanted to know. A small bit of her was even jealous he'd made such a breakthrough in a single afternoon when she felt as if she'd been struggling with Zack forever. It was like her grandpa who would walk into the room, glance at the puzzle she was working on and find the piece that had eluded her for an hour. You were happy something was accomplished, but it stung that it wasn't you that pulled it off. *You asked him to help*, she reminded herself. *Just be happy that he has*.

Sawyer leaned against the counter. It was the first time he didn't look in such a hurry to leave. "I'm not really sure. The golf thing didn't go that well, actually. I just took him into the clubhouse for a soda when his frustration got the better of him."

"You must have said something important. He kept muttering to himself about 'new' and 'lousy.'"

That seemed to prick the man's memory. "Well, I did tell him that most new things feel lousy at first."

That seemed like a terrible way to view the world. "How on earth did that help?"

"Have you ever noticed your tendency to be wildly overoptimistic?"

That was a loaded question. And a far cry from their usual morning small talk over his daily coffee. Molly's spine stiffened in a defensive response. "Are you saying I'm too happy to help my son?" The urge to spill everything wrong with her life—the divorce and the cancer and the sleepless nights—rose up out of nowhere.

Sawyer seemed to realize he'd touched a nerve. "I'm saying you don't think like him. I get how he thinks. Maybe he just needed to know he wasn't the only person in the world who thinks the way he does." He gave her something close to a grin. "You can be a bit of a flood of sunshine, if you hadn't noticed."

That statement just might take the cake for the world's most backhanded compliment. And from Sawyer Bradshaw. Life was chock-full of surprises this week.

Molly offered the thing she should have said from

the first: "Thank you. For whatever you did for Zack. It means the world to me."

"It was just a root beer, Molly."

Her attention always caught in a strange way when he used her name. He was such a closed person that any little slip of connection like that stood out. "You're wrong, Sawyer. It was a whole lot more than that. And I'm grateful."

He looked as if he was turning to go, and Molly found herself wanting to make him stay just a little longer. She wanted to know why he never really smiled. Why he seemed eager to shrink from the world. She wanted to know more about this man who'd fostered an impossible connection to her son without any effort. She wanted to know why God had nudged her—no, shoved her—into putting this man into Zack's life. Nothing about it made sense, but clearly it had some purpose. She just couldn't see that purpose yet.

"What about the golf part? The way he looked at the clubs last night, I couldn't tell if he thought they were friends or enemies."

Sawyer let loose a small laugh at that. "I could name a dozen golfers who feel the same way. He's just—" he looked up at the ceiling as if the right word was hanging there "—clumsy with them. For now. He knows what needs to happen, but he can't quite find the coordination to make it happen."

Zack never looked as if he was at home in his body. "He's always been a bit of an 'indoor cat,' as my grandpa used to say. That's part of the reason golf might work, according to Mrs. Hollings. A place to burn off all the physical energy of those anxieties." Rather than voice her fears that this strange experiment might not work, might just pile on to the failures Zack saw for himself, she began wiping down the counter. Being so quick to get her hopes up made for a roller coaster of an emotional ride parenting Zack, always had.

"Did you ask him if he still wants to come next time?"

She'd been dreading it. She'd be so elated if he continued on, and so disappointed if he didn't. "Not yet."

Sawyer gave her as pointed a look as he'd ever had. "You gotta."

"What if he says no?" She wished the question didn't sound so desperate.

"Maybe you could just be happy you got an attempted root beer out of the deal and try again another time."

Right there was Molly's trouble with the world. She was never satisfied with small victories. She was always grasping at marvels and delights. Life was too short for anything less. "Easier said than done."

After a moment, she lamented, "I don't want him to quit now." She felt her cheeks heat with embarrassment at the emotion in her voice.

His eyes softened. "If it helps, neither do I."

That rarest of admissions from him did help. Immensely. Some days it felt as if she needed to know the whole world was pulling for Zack as hard as she was. Molly pushed her chin up and straightened her shoulders. "I *am* happy for the attempted root beer."

He nodded his approval at how she'd given his own words back to him. "There you go."

"Do you think…" She hesitated to ask, but it felt

like an easier yes to get from Zack than another trip to Mountain Vista. "Could we do the next lesson in our backyard? It might feel like less pressure."

Sawyer's face registered surprise and doubt. She couldn't really blame him, given that she'd just essentially invited him over. He'd never struck her as an "invite over" kind of guy.

"He said you just painted a big circle on the grass," she went on. "I'd be willing to do that. And now, it seems, we have root beer in the fridge." Why was she trying so hard?

"Why don't you ask Zack which he'd like?"

As dodges went, that one was pretty effective. Molly had people over all the time. She was a people person, always inviting people to things—church, home, committees, events. Why this particular invitation seemed to hold so much weight, she couldn't guess.

Except that this was Zack, and every little thing mattered when it was Zack.

"I can do that. I'll let you know what he says."

Sawyer did finally turn to go this time. "Do that."

"He said he liked it," Molly called after him, determined to end this on an up note. "Not the root beer, but the golf."

"Did he?" Sawyer raised one eyebrow at the pronouncement. Was that satisfaction that flashed across his features?

"Well, not in so many words," she amended. "He's not like that. But I was expecting his usual collection of 'I hate it' groans, and I didn't get that. To me, that adds up to an 'I like it.'" The explanation sounded ridiculous now that she said it out loud. "You did a good thing there, Sawyer." She got the sense he needed to hear that.

He made no reply, just nodded his head in acknowledgment and ducked out the door.

Molly watched him through the windows. She was almost certain she didn't imagine the smile that crept across his face as he got into his truck.

What do you know? Sawyer Bradshaw *did* have the capacity to smile. The satisfaction she took from that made her stand a little taller. Perhaps while Zack learned to golf, Sawyer might learn to smile more. It sounded like a preposterous idea that just might succeed.

# Chapter Four

"Hi, everybody," Molly called out as she settled herself at the table with her three brunch companions. "Sorry I'm a bit late."

"You're usually the first one here," Molly's friend, fellow single mom and choir soprano Tessa Kennedy remarked. "Everything okay with Zack?"

Molly reached for a napkin and took a sip of the orange juice already waiting for her. "Hopefully. It's too early to know for sure, but we might finally have hit on a solution... I think." No doubt Tessa had already ordered for her since the friends had been meeting for a late breakfast once a week for over a year. They knew she never had anything but blueberry pancakes. "I almost invited someone to join us." She had actually considered inviting Sawyer to breakfast. The church choir brunch, however, seemed so beyond his nature. She'd already asked enough of the man.

Marilyn Walker, mom of twins and member of the alto section, looked behind Molly toward the door. "Who?"

"Zack's new golf teacher. I think he needed to make more friends."

Every person at the table looked startled.

"You actually went through with it?" Her friend Tessa balked. "You asked the guy from The Depot to teach Zack golf?"

Walt Peters managed a laugh. "You've had some doozies, but this might be your zaniest idea yet."

Molly lifted her chin. "You wouldn't say that if I told you Zack actually tried a new flavor of soda last night."

That brought even more startled looks from around the table.

"You can't argue with a result like that," her friend Marilyn admitted. "But come on, you think everyone needs more friends. Choir would be half the size it is if it weren't for you inviting people. Solos, too."

The Solos single mothers' Bible study had been a lifeline for Molly during all the struggles with Zack. Tessa had been a member since before Molly had joined, and although Marilyn was now happily remarried, no one had the heart to kick her out. "Hey, some weeks, choir and Solos are the only things keeping me sane. Well, choir, Solos and these pancakes." Molly gave a dramatic sigh of anticipation as the server set a glorious plate of blueberry pancakes in front of her. "Pancakes and coffee are the answer to almost everything."

Tessa dug into her omelet. "You sound like Greg. The answer to everything in my son's life is 'What do we have to eat?'"

"Can he sing?" asked Walt. The older gentleman was both the owner of the local pet shop and the deepest voice in the choir. "We need more baritones."

"I didn't ask him if he could sing," Molly replied. "I don't know him that well."

"You don't know him well enough to ask him if he can sing, but you're letting him spend time with Zack?" Tessa teased. "What do you know about him?"

"He comes in after his night shift for coffee every morning like clockwork." She doused her pancakes in Gwen's luscious blueberry syrup. Life didn't afford her many luxuries, but this was one of her favorites. The good food and great company always fortified her for the second half of her day dealing with the under-caffeinated, impatient customers of The Depot.

She had held back one crucial detail, but it was time to get it out in the open. "He works security at Mountain Vista."

The frowns and scowls around the table were pretty much what she expected. As if her comment had directed their gazes, her companions glanced over to the two tables of Mountain Vista guests in the dining room right now. They were often easy to spot: fancy sportswear, designer sunglasses and a healthy dose of "how quaint" attitude. She tried never to judge them, but the way they often looked down their noses at townspeople made it hard.

"There isn't enough money in the world to make me take a job there," Marilyn said. Before she married Wyatt Walker, her late husband had been involved in shady dealings with the resort. It was a revelation that only soured local opinions further.

"Sawyer's never talked about it, but I get the sense he's not there by choice."

"Who would be?" Tessa replied.

Molly recalled Sawyer's dark brown hair and the

strikingly lighter, near-golden tone of his eyes. There was hardly any light in those eyes, despite their glowing hue. The man always looked as if he was just waiting till some disaster came for him. That was why she knew he would understand Zack. They were kindred spirits. Despite the dubious looks of her friends, Molly's gut told her Sawyer was the right person to teach Zack.

"Are you sure this is a good idea?" Marilyn asked carefully.

Molly repeated all the reasons she'd given both Pastor Newton and Sawyer. "Zack needs something not too physical that he can do solo at first. He needs someone very low-key who will be okay with him failing at it at first. So, no fancy golf pro. He's the right guy for this, I'm sure of it."

Walt didn't look especially convinced, either. "Are things going that badly at school that you'd try something like this?"

It was the one question she didn't really want to answer, even with these friends. Fighting Zack's anxiety was like shadowboxing. So many attempts to help him felt like clutching at thin air. Was this outlandish idea just a product of her own frustration? Her inability to make any headway with Zack? Was she reading too much into a simple choice of soda?

"We'd do anything to help Zack, you know we would." Marilyn's eyes held sympathy, not judgment, but Molly couldn't help being envious of how cheery Mari's twin girls were. They'd been through a huge trauma in the loss of their father, but somehow they'd come out okay, while the pain of his father's abandonment seemed to wound Zack every single day.

"I know it's a wild idea, but I've tried all the logical ones already."

"I'll try and talk to him again if you'd like," Walt offered. The sweet, grandfatherly man had tried so many times to make some sort of connection with Zack, but it just hadn't clicked. Pastor Newton had done the same, but with no better results. Molly was sure there was a happy Zack in there somewhere buried under all the storm of worries; she just didn't know how to coax it out.

"You've overcome so much, Molly." Tessa was always quick with an encouraging word. "You'll show Zack how to overcome this, too. You're coming up on a benchmark, aren't you?"

Molly hoisted her orange juice. "Two years remission next week."

"Amen and alleluia to that," Marilyn said as everyone around the table toasted Molly's second year of being cancer-free.

"I love Zack so much, but he just…stumps me. It's like he lives on a whole different, darker planet."

"And you're one of the most optimistic people I know," Marilyn continued. "Of course Zack's fragility stumps you."

Too many people used that word to describe Zack: fragile. She never liked it, even if it was accurate. It always made her feel as if Zack was hopelessly bound to be crushed by a cruel world.

"He's a turtle of a soul," Walt said. "He pulls deep into his shell for protection. It's not about how they're parented. It's just what turtles do."

Molly wasn't sure she bought into Walt's pet shop

wisdom. "So I'm sending my turtle to a golf course. What does that make me?"

Walt smiled. "You, kiddo, are a unicorn. One of a kind, scattering hopeful rainbows all over the place."

"You mean imaginary," Molly teased back.

"Nonsense," Tessa said. "There's been a unicorn on the carousel for years. Real as can be."

The coffee shop was in the center of town next to Wander Canyon's beloved carousel. One of the best parts about working at The Depot was getting the chance to see children and families grab a bit of joy on the un-usual carousel filled with all kinds of animals—except ponies. Who couldn't love living in a town known for its whimsical carousel? Some of her favorite customers were the riders—young and old—who stopped in the shop afterward, still shiny-faced and smiling, for a cof-fee or a cookie or hot chocolate. It was a daily reminder of how happiness was possible. Even when it seemed a far reach for Zack.

"Remember," Walt said, pointing at Molly with a slice of toast, "the tortoise won the race over the hare. Who knows? Maybe learning golf really will help Zack find his feet in this world. He's got too many people praying for him to not get there somehow."

Molly stared into the blue swirls of her pancake syrup. "Well, everyone pray that this wild idea works. This unicorn is running out of rainbows."

# Chapter Five

Sawyer stared at the collection of plastic piping in the Wander Canyon hardware store on Thursday afternoon. He was trying to work out the best way to build a make-shift golf hole in Molly's backyard.

How he had let Molly talk him into doing this at her house rather than the safety of the grass behind the golf course, he'd never know. That woman had massive powers of persuasion, and he just couldn't seem to find a way to say no to even the oddest of her requests. And, if he was honest, Sawyer harbored a small curiosity as to what Molly's house would look like. Bright riots of color like her clothes and jewelry? Or soft tones and textures like her voice and eyes?

He'd thought about just borrowing the hardware from the resort, but then he'd have to explain to someone what he was doing. He'd already gone into way too much of an explanation already to get Zack his clubs.

Sawyer grabbed a short section of plastic plumbing piping and brought it to the counter. "Can you cut me off a four-inch segment? Maybe two of them?"

The man, whose patch on his shirt identified him as Leo, eyed him. "No can do. Gonna have to buy at least a foot."

"Okay, then, three bits of four-inch length."

Leo nodded. "Whatcha building?"

"I guess now I'm building a *three*-hole golf course." Why had he just admitted that? And how had he gone from consenting to visit Molly's house to doing landscaping?

"Gonna give those idiots up at Mountain Vista a run for their money, eh?" the old man chuckled as he marked off lines on the pipe with a ruler and a pen.

Sawyer chose not to reply. Some weeks every day showed him a reason why folks here held no love for his employer. That was okay, he felt no loyalty to them, either. He didn't feel much of anything these days.

It struck him, just then, that he'd never heard Molly join in the chorus of disapproval for Mountain Vista. In fact, he'd never heard her say anything bad about anybody. *Huh.* He'd sort of forgotten people like that still existed. Just another way Molly Kane was unique. And memorable.

"I got an idea." Leo stopped marking the pipe and looked past Sawyer's shoulder farther into the store. "Buy a couple of four-inch plastic flowerpots. Sink 'em right in the ground. It'd be cheaper. Drainage built right in."

Maybe talking to people had its advantages. "That's a pretty good idea."

Leo smiled. "C'mon, I'll show you where they are."

Wander Canyon's hardware store wasn't so large that Sawyer couldn't have found his way into the garden aisle on his own. Leo kept up a stream of friendly chatter as he moved through the aisles, stopping in front of a young man and a little boy Sawyer guessed to be a few years younger than Zack.

"Jake!" Leo called to the young man. "How's married life treating you?" With a knowing wink Leo said, "Newlywed. Car guy. Runs the construction business in town."

Without Sawyer's permission, Leo proceeded to tell this Jake all about Sawyer's plans to build a three-hole golf course. Sawyer couldn't entirely be sure Leo was laughing with him, or at him. Maybe talking to people *wasn't* such a good idea.

Jake held out a hand to Sawyer. "Do I know you?"

It'd be far too rude to say, "No, and I'd like to keep it that way," so Sawyer simply said, "New in town." He hoped, but rather doubted, that his answer would suffice.

"We're building a tank stand," spouted the little boy beside him with a grin that showed a missing tooth. "For my turtles."

"Just sitting on the bookshelf is so last year," Jake joked. "The cool turtles all want their own stands now."

"Just like you want your own putting green, huh?" Leo said to Sawyer.

"It's not for me," Sawyer replied, then immediately regretted the response. It would only lead to…

"Well, who's it for?" Leo squinted at him. "Not too many golfers in town on account of…"

Sawyer cut him off. "A little boy." He looked at the child next to Jake. "A bit older than you, actually." Hoping that would satisfy Leo's curiosity, Sawyer tried to continue his progress toward the stacks of pots and other garden supplies.

"What boy in this town wants to take up golf?" Leo seemed scandalized at the thought.

"Leo," Jake said. "You don't have to know everything to help the guy." Jake threw an apologetic look in Sawyer's direction.

"It's odd, that's all I'm saying," Leo explained.

"I'm a baseball man, myself," Jake added. "We've got a great men's team if you'd be interested. Our catcher broke his ankle last month and the playoffs are looking sketchy without him."

Did everyone try to recruit everyone for everything in this town? Sawyer had spent most of his adult life in Denver and rarely been invited to anything. He'd already been asked to more meals and events in his time in Wander than that whole time in Denver. His tactic of hiding in a small town had some serious flaws.

"Not my thing," Sawyer replied, wishing a man of his size could more easily hide in the store's narrow aisles. "Thanks anyway."

"Well, if you change your mind, just find me at Car-San Construction."

"Or Emmom at the preschool," the boy chimed in.

"Little Cole's stepmom runs the local preschool," Leo explained. Evidently Leo felt introductions were a part of customer service.

Sawyer grabbed three plastic flowerpots off the shelf and wished he'd stuck with the lengths of pipe. "These'll be great. Thanks for the help, Leo." He managed a nod to Jake and Cole. "Nice to meet you."

Sawyer was finished with paying for his purchase

and halfway out the door before he realized he'd just engaged in small talk. Him, chatting with the locals in the hardware store. How small-town could you get?

Wander Canyon was getting to him, and he wasn't sure he liked where this was heading.

Molly looked at her watch. At this rate, she was going to be late for meeting Sawyer at the house. He was a detail guy, and based on his regular appearances at The Depot, very punctual.

She looked around the carousel house, where the meeting she was in was still going strong. The Wander Canyon Carousel was celebrating its fortieth anniversary in two weeks, and the town was holding a big festival to celebrate. The planning committee—all parents of children young enough to adore the ride, although Wander residents of any age were devoted to it—had already let their children choose which ride they would recreate as a wagon to ride in a Saturday morning parade. Zack had finally consented to participate, and she had been waiting almost an hour for Zack to decide his animal. These kinds of decisions always took Zack a long time.

Pulling out her phone, she texted Sawyer. Can you meet me at the carousel instead? Not quite done with my meeting here. Honestly, she worried that if she let Sawyer wait for her at the house too long, he might leave. After a second, she added another text. Big red building right next to the coffee shop. She probably didn't have to do that. He'd know where the carousel was because everybody knew where the Wander Canyon Carousel was.

She tried not to read too much into the long pause before he replied, OK.

As it turned out, Zack was still debating between the hippo and the kangaroo when Sawyer arrived. Molly was surprised to see his jaw drop when he pushed through the doors into the large circular room that held the carousel.

She left Zack to his pondering and walked over to greet Sawyer. "Don't tell me you've never seen the Wander Canyon Carousel."

One eyebrow lowered at her. "Why would I come in here?"

"Because *everybody* comes in here." For a split second her brain tried to concoct an image of serious Sawyer Bradshaw atop a carousel animal, but she couldn't fathom it. "Even the grown-ups ride the carousel in this town."

Sawyer looked supremely relieved that the amusement wasn't turned on at the moment. He was right— she couldn't have resisted trying to get him on for a ride if it had been running.

Sawyer stuffed his hands in his pockets. "What kind of meeting happens on a carousel?"

Molly laughed. "Not *on* the carousel, *about* it. This year is the carousel's fortieth anniversary, and there's a big to-do in town in two weeks to celebrate. Zack's picking his animal." She allowed herself a small sigh. "It's taking a long time for him to choose."

"Two weeks? Are there any left to pick from?"

"Thankfully, they're not assigned. There are way more kids than animals, so each child can choose whichever animal they want."

Sawyer stared at the collection of beautifully carved wooden animals. Molly waited for him to realize what made it so distinct.

"Where are the horses?" he asked, looking as stumped as anyone else when they first saw the town's pride and joy.

"There aren't any."

"A carousel with no ponies?"

"Yep. But we've got just about everything else."

Sawyer scanned the colorful set of animals behind her, gave a double take then almost laughed. She liked that they could have a conversation with some ease now. More than coffee orders, at least. She found herself wanting to get to know him, to peel off some of that defensive silence he spent so much energy keeping up. "Our carousel probably has mounts you've never seen before."

"You're right about that. Can't say I've ever seen a carousel gorilla."

Molly had to smile that he'd noticed the gorilla. More than one person in Wander had a theory that whichever animal someone chose said a lot about their personality. She would have easily guessed Sawyer to go for the gorilla. Or maybe the porcupine.

"My favorite has always been the peacock," she offered.

"Figures," he said. It wasn't an unkind remark. In fact, she could almost rate it as a compliment when he added, "Suits you."

They watched Zack standing in front of the two animals, twisting a rubber band around his fingers and shifting his feet. "I take it Zack can't choose a favorite?" It touched her that his voice held no hint of judgment or impatience.

"It's not a big deal, but you know Zack." She shifted her handbag to her other shoulder and checked her watch again. "Lots of things are big deals to him."

Sawyer nodded. *He gets it*, Molly thought to herself. *So few people do, but he does.*

Sawyer scratched his chin, thinking. "So what does he choose it for?"

"People are building floats of sorts for a parade down Main Street. However you want to do it is up to you. Bicycles, wagons, tractors, baby strollers, shopping carts, you name it. As long as it can move, it's in the parade."

"What are you going to use?" he asked.

That was a good question. "Who knows? Right now I'm just trying to get us past step one, which is choosing an animal."

They stood together for a quiet moment, waiting on Zack. It wasn't uncomfortable, but it did give her a new sense of how tall he was. If security guards ought to be big, solid men, he definitely fit the bill.

Despite his punctuality, Sawyer didn't seem to be in the hurry she feared. Molly stole a glance at the man next to her, shifting her eyes away quickly when she caught him stealing a glance at her. She shook off the little spark of something in the air between them, convincing herself it was awkwardness.

Then Sawyer surprised Molly by walking over and crouching down to Zack's height. Something told her to stay put, to let Sawyer have a try, moving Zack toward a decision when she hadn't been able to.

"Can't pick?" Sawyer asked. Molly was so pleased to hear no hint of pressure in his question.

"They're both good," Zack replied. He looked at Sawyer with worried eyes. "What if I pick the wrong one? What if I build the hippo and end up wishing I'd built the kangaroo?"

"I see your point," Sawyer replied.

Molly's heart pinched at Sawyer's response. Steve—and others, for that matter, but especially Steve—dismissed Zack's worries. They were small to others, she got that. But they were large to Zack. For all Sawyer's gruffness, the man's sad outlook somehow gave him a window into Zack's world. One her own frustrations and worries wouldn't let her see.

"But I gotta choose," Zack practically moaned, the rubber band twisting tighter between his fingers.

Sawyer scrubbed a hand across his chin. "Well, let's just take this apart and look at the pieces." When Zack's eyes popped wide, Sawyer revised, "The decision, not the carousel."

He scooted over to sit on the carousel platform, now stationary, in between the two animals Zack was considering. Patting the platform, he invited Zack to do the same.

Molly stood there looking at the pairing of the man and the boy. On the one hand, her heart ached for the fact that it was not Zack's father guiding him through this decision. Not that she missed Steve—the love between them had long since cooled. And although she would have stayed, prayed and fought to save the marriage, Steve had no interest in doing so.

No, the scene in front of her made her ache with

mourning for the father Zack had lost. Not to death or distance or even just divorce, but to heartbreaking indifference. As if Zack was a complicated car Steve was no longer interested in bothering to maintain.

"Seems to me the point of all this is to have fun building a…" Sawyer looked to Molly to fill in the blank.

"An animal for the parade."

Sawyer looked at Zack. "Is that it?"

"I guess."

Did Sawyer notice that Zack had stopped twisting the rubber band so hard? Did the man realize how his surprising connection with Zack calmed her son in ways she still couldn't explain?

"So, if you have fun building the hippo, that's what's supposed to happen, right?"

Zack wrinkled his small brow. "I guess."

"And if you have fun building the kangaroo, then that's what's supposed to happen, too, right?"

"Maybe."

"So either one is an okay choice. I don't think you'll have any more fun building the hippo than building the kangaroo. The thing is, will you have fun doing it? That's totally up to you. I mean, if you can have fun with pizza golf than you can have fun doing pretty much anything."

"I can have fun doing pretty much anything" was about as foreign a statement as Molly could imagine coming out of her son's mouth. Or Sawyer's, for that matter. Yet Zack seemed to accept it.

She watched Sawyer lean back until he had both animals in his view. It seemed such an uncharacteristic stance for him. Sawyer so often seemed folded in on himself, and yet here he seemed comfortable taking up space, expansive, even. There was a protective air about him, something close to a command, that she'd not seen before. It touched her that Sawyer wielded that protection on behalf of Zack. There was clearly so much more to this man than met the eye. There was a deep history, likely a deep pain, that kept him closed off.

And yet here was Zack, slowly prying that thick wall of protection open. Zack was so special, if people just took the time with him the way Sawyer did.

"I don't know..." Zack said slowly, not entirely convinced by Sawyer's logic. After all, logic rarely worked against fear and anxiety—she knew that too well.

She didn't know, either. Not about which animal to choose, but about the man in front of her. She liked to think she knew people, that she had God-given instincts about them, but that wasn't the same as knowing them. She felt a gentle pull toward Sawyer that she neither welcomed nor understood.

It was becoming something more than gratitude. Not to say she wasn't grateful for the connection he seemed to have with Zack. She was enormously grateful for that, even if she couldn't explain it. This was something else. Something *man-woman*, something more instinctual than a mother being glad for a solution. Something she hadn't felt in a long time.

And something that was definitely not a good idea. Now wasn't the time to rock the boat for either her or Zack, especially in that department. *Definitely not now*, Molly reminded herself as she watched Zack talk to Sawyer.

"I'll feel lousy after I choose," Zack said.

There was that word again. *Lousy.* It wasn't a word she used. And yet Zack had used it in a dozen unexpected places recently, but couldn't—or wouldn't—explain why.

Sawyer didn't seem surprised by the comment at all. "New choice, new project, lousy feeling. They sometimes go together, right?"

*It came from him*, Molly remembered. A bit grumpy and extreme, but the same could be said of Sawyer. She couldn't deny that the word had touched some useful nerve in Zack.

"And once it's not new, it probably won't feel lousy, right?"

Zack nodded. It wasn't at all how she would describe her son's anxieties, but what did that matter in the face of the connection it made with Zack?

The room was silent for so long even Molly began to feel anxious. Zack kept looking back and forth between animals, hands working the rubber band, little shoulders in a fretful scrunch. *Send a bucket of patience, right now, Lord.* Molly could almost laugh at the contrast in her prayer.

Zack suddenly stood, planted his feet as if the pronouncement might knock him over, and said, "Hippo."

Molly didn't even realize she'd been holding her breath.

"I like it," Sawyer said, acknowledging the decision without making too much of it. She was just about to make too much of it, she realized.

There was something special about this man. Something unique and perfectly suited to Zack. Molly just needed to make sure Sawyer stayed unique and perfectly suited to Zack, and Zack alone.

Not to her.

# Chapter Six

Sawyer waved hello to Zack as he hauled his little set of clubs out of Molly's car. He caught himself, stunned at the impulsive friendly gesture. Sawyer wasn't a wave hello kind of guy—at least he hadn't been lately.

Molly got out of the car with one of those cardboard cup trays holding a trio of to-go cups from The Depot in her hand.

"You don't work on Saturdays," he said, realizing after the fact that the comment revealed he knew her usual schedule. She probably saw that as creepy, and she'd be right.

"But *you* do, so I figured it was the least I could do." They'd spent too much time at the carousel house Friday night to install the makeshift holes in Molly's backyard, so Sawyer had suggested Zack come by the resort for today's lesson after Sawyer finished his night shift. "One double-shot Americano for you, one hot chocolate extra whipped cream and sprinkles for Zack, and a raspberry mocha latte for me."

Did people choose to have so sunny a disposition

this early in the morning, or was it genetic? He never could seem to make such an outlook happen before noon, if ever.

"Zack, why don't you put your clubs over by Mr. Sawyer's office while I give him his coffee."

Zack gave Sawyer a look that roughly translated to "I get she wants to talk to you without me," before taking his cocoa and clubs and trotting off to the spot where they'd had their first lesson. *Kid's smarter than I realized*, Sawyer thought to himself. *I should remember that.*

Molly handed him the coffee. Hot and delicious, it beat the "drink it just because it's caffeine" coffee in the resort's security office by a mile. Coffee was such a small detail, but she took enormous care with how she treated it. How she treated him. It was one of the things he liked most about her. She was always so full of kindness.

"Thank you," Molly said in an earnest gush. "I mean it, really."

"How'd it go?" He wasn't ready to admit to Molly that he'd spent half his shift wondering how the carousel animal decision had sat with Zack. In the predawn hours of his shift he'd envisioned Zack lying in bed, wide-eyed and sleepless with worry over the hippo-or-kangaroo question. Nor would he admit that occasionally those thoughts would wander to Molly, who he could guess was equally sleepless and worried. It seemed unfair that she had to fret so much about her son's worrying.

"Let's just say I heard the word *lousy* a few times

last night," she admitted. "Never thought I'd come to see that word as a good one."

The woman in front of him was such a relentless optimist she probably never used a word like *lousy* to describe anything.

"He didn't back out of the choice or anything, did he?" He actually craved the small victory of helping Zack make and stick with the decision. To give something back for all that Molly didn't even realize she gave him. That *was* new, and it didn't feel lousy.

She pressed her lips together. "Well, it was a bit shaky there for a while. But—" she cast her glance in the direction Zack had gone "—he worked through it. That's huge. You have to know how huge that is."

He suspected that on some level, but the gratitude on Molly's face confirmed it. *Heartwarming* wasn't really a word he normally used, but the look on her sunny features did raise up a little warmth in his chest.

"Glad to hear it. Let's hope today doesn't mess that up." A bout of frustration over figuring out golf could undo Zack's tiny burst of confidence. Sawyer knew that, and it reminded him how far out of his league this impromptu golf teacher thing was.

As he turned to go, Molly grabbed his free arm. Both of them froze, startled by the contact. They'd never actually touched before, and casual as the gesture was, it seemed absurdly important that they just had. He felt the press of her fingers zing the whole way up his arm.

She pulled her hand away. "I just thought you ought to know. Zack's dad… He's not…he's not in his life the way he should be."

Sawyer wasn't sure why she felt he needed to know

that, but he didn't offer a response. He was still a little too stunned by the memory of her hand touching his skin.

"Steve couldn't understand Zack's personality. He looked down on Zack's fears. In the end he...wasn't kind."

A burn of anger rose in Sawyer's gut. *Talk about lousy.*

"Just...be careful. You've been great so far and you get him, and I'm so glad for that, but he's...fragile. In that way, I mean."

She was pleading for him not to hurt her son. It was compelling and terrifying at the same time. Sawyer suddenly found himself in higher stakes than he wanted, unable to back out now. He had a mile-high mountain of regrets in his life, and the last thing he wanted was to add Zack Kane to that pile.

A nobler man probably would have made some grand promise, but Sawyer wasn't that man. "I get it," was all he could say, even though Molly's expression told him that probably wasn't enough.

She took it, though, forcing a smile and a nod. "Okay, then. Thanks. I'm going to run to the store and I'll be back at ten thirty to pick him up."

"We'll be here." The exchange felt too ordinary for what had just been communicated, but Zack was waiting.

Molly toasted him with her coffee, and he toasted back, feeling ridiculous. Then Sawyer turned toward the little patch of green behind the maintenance shed. Somehow, he was going to have to avoid squashing Zack's confidence while teaching him the often-humbling sport of golf. A tall order, indeed.

Zack stood waiting for him.

Sawyer drew his shoulders back in a "let's get right to it" stance. "I'm thinking today won't feel as new, so we'll do better." While it veered dangerously toward Molly's brand of optimism, Sawyer felt compelled to at least try to set a good intention. "And we've got decent drinks, so there's that."

"What's so great about coffee anyway?" Zack asked. "Everybody makes a big deal about it."

Sawyer had to think about that for a minute. "Do you ever have trouble waking up in the morning?"

Zack blinked. "No."

"Then I'm not sure I can explain it to you." He held up the cup. "It helps me to wake up. Or stay awake. What your mom makes tastes really good, too, but it's mostly about the thing in coffee—caffeine—that makes it such a big deal. To grown-ups, at least. Caffeine's not for kids. You guys come with your own energy."

"Mom says that all the time. Dad used to…"

The kid's mouth snapped shut so fast Sawyer felt it in his gut. That alone would have told him his father was a sore subject even if Molly hadn't given him a warning.

Maybe not *right to it* this morning. Sawyer sat down on the curb and motioned for Zack to do the same.

"Your dad used to what?" When Zack hesitated, he added, "It's okay to say it to me."

"He said Mom made the best coffee in the world." His soft tone held a whole world of loss inside it. It stung even more that Sawyer had had the same thought once or twice. Molly made fabulous coffee.

"Your mom does make really good coffee." While it seemed a dangerous thing to do, Sawyer couldn't help but ask, "Do you miss him?"

Zack scuffed his shoe against the asphalt and stared down at the hot chocolate. "I miss him from earlier. From when he was nice. When he and Mom didn't yell at each other. I don't miss the yelling."

This seemed way more important than the correct grip on a golf club. "Is he far away now?" It seemed the safest way to ask about the role Zack's dad had in his current life.

"I never talk to him." Five words that sounded as if they weighed a thousand pounds.

"That has to feel lousy." There was no making light of a fact like that, no way to gloss over a hole like that in a boy's life.

"Mom tells me all kinds of reasons. I know they're not true."

How had things gone so deep so fast with this little boy he hardly knew? The connection struck a fear—and a responsibility—so strong in Sawyer it was nearly a physical sensation. The same "run toward the danger" impulse that lived in the heart of every cop. The fact that he no longer wore a badge hadn't changed that, just put it to sleep for a while. Waking it up wasn't at all comfortable.

"You're a really smart kid, you know that, right? Sometimes it's not much fun to be that smart, is it?"

"It's lousy some days." The word had become a bond between them.

"Do you talk to your mom about it?" It seemed the right thing to say.

Zack gave him such a dubious look that Sawyer had to tamp down a laugh. "C'mon. Mom? She gets all weird about it."

"Well, yeah, I could see how that happens. But that's what moms do. They worry about stuff." He started to say something about how his mom always worried about him on the force, but he didn't want to go down that road right now. "But they also care, so it's a good trade-off." If what Molly said was true, Zack's dad had stopped caring.

"How'd you learn to play golf?" Evidently Zack was ready to switch off the tender topic.

Unfortunately, that was the wrong question to make that switch. Still, the kid deserved the respect of the truth. "My dad, actually. I suppose I can blame him for what a lousy golfer I am."

"So I'm gonna be lousy, too?" Sawyer was pleased to see it was a joke, not a complaint.

"I hope not. You're smarter than me, and golf is as much about how you think as about how you swing."

He wondered if Molly found Zack's frown adorable or heartbreaking. Likely both. "I think a lot. Mom says sometimes too much."

Sawyer stood up. "Yeah, thinking too much will get you every time. Let's see if we can't nail that swing today. Tiny ball, big circle on the grass, piece of cake, right?"

"Maybe."

Well, then, *maybe* would have to do.


Molly stared at her phone, waiting on the too-long silence after asking Sawyer the question.

She'd gone too far. She was always going too far, but the smile on Zack's face as she drove him home from the golf lesson had driven her to it.

Actually, it was more accurate to say Zack's nonstop begging had driven her to it, but Molly wasn't sure Sawyer would see it that way.

"He hasta come, Mom. He hasta," Zack had pleaded all the way home. She couldn't make her son embrace the idea that maybe he could practice a few more days before they sank the flowerpots to make a tiny golf course in their backyard. Zack would not entertain the idea that she—or anyone else—could help with this. It had to be Sawyer, and it had to be tonight.

The connection between those two had sprung up so hard and so fast Molly wasn't quite sure it was safe. Or even wise. Then again, when had Zack thrown himself into anything with this kind of enthusiasm? Who could have guessed the ability to knock a small white ball into a spray-painted orange circle on a patch of grass could work such wonders?

"So will you come?" she asked—pleaded—into her cell phone.

"I need a few hours' sleep," Sawyer replied wearily. "Somebody made me stay up late already today."

She *had* gone too far. "I'm so sorry. I shouldn't have asked. It's just that Zack is…" What? Excited? Begging? Bordering on obsessive?

"I just meant I can't come now," he said, and Molly's chest flooded with relief. "Like six maybe?"

"Six would be wonderful. I'll make you dinner." Molly wanted to bite the words back out of the air the moment she said them. Two dinners with the man in as many weeks? "Wander's always watching" was a common saying in this town for good reason. Tongues might wag.

"Mr. Sawyer's coming for dinner?" Zack's delighted voice came from behind her. She'd thought he'd been outside.

Sawyer gave a small, low laugh. He had heard Zack, as well. "No backing out now, is there?"

"No?" It was more of an asking-for-permission-to-impose than it was an answer.

"He's that happy about today, is he?" Was that a touch of wonder she heard in his voice? It sounded so out of place she couldn't be sure.

"Ecstatic," she replied.

"What's that mean?" Zack asked.

"It means really happy."

"Yeah, that," Zack confirmed.

"Thank you so much. Six will be perfect. Do I need to find any tools or anything? Golf balls?" Earlier, he'd explained his idea of sinking plastic flowerpots as golf holes into spots in her backyard. It seemed like a good idea, but she had no idea how such a thing was done.

Sawyer almost gave a real laugh. Almost. "I'll pick up what I need from the course." He yawned, and she wondered if 11:00 a.m. was the equivalent of three o'clock in the morning for someone who worked nights.

"Thank you." She tried to make the two words full of all the gratitude she felt.

"Glad he's happy. I'll see you at six."

When Molly put down the phone, Zack was staring at the clock on the wall. "That's *seven whole hours* from now." He made it sound like seven months.

"That should give you more than enough time to get your homework and Saturday chores done before tee time."

Zack scrunched up his face as if he was preparing to launch into his usual resistance. Molly calculated whether or not to pick the phone back up. She hadn't had leverage like this to win Zack's cooperation in years.

She never had to move her hand. Zack simply nodded and headed toward the dishwasher to empty it without even being asked.

*I don't know how You did it, Lord, but I sure am glad You did.* If a heart could smile, that was what the glow in Molly's chest felt like. *Now if You could just get me through the next seven hours, I'd be obliged.*

By six o'clock, Molly couldn't rightly say if she was grateful or daunted by the anticipation Zack had shown all afternoon. The investment her son seemed to now have in Sawyer Bradshaw worried her. Enough people in Zack's life had disappointed him, and she didn't want Sawyer to be the next. It felt dangerous to entrust her son's rare enthusiasm on someone so dark and gruff.

On the other hand, her own instincts about the man told her there was so much more to Sawyer than what he showed the world. Whatever it was that Zack felt, she had to admit to feeling a little bit of it, as well.

"Hi," Zack practically shouted the moment he ran to the door and yanked it open.

"Hi, yourself," Sawyer replied. The man's questioning eyes told her he found Zack's excitement as baffling as she did.

"Mom let me spray-paint the grass," Zack said, pulling Sawyer toward the backyard before he'd even had a chance to set down the canvas bag he was holding.

Molly caught Sawyer's raised eyebrow as he was dragged through the kitchen toward the back door. "By three o'clock I caved to just about anything," she admitted.

She had, in fact, found a can of red spray paint and allowed Zack to "draw" a trio of two-foot circles on the grass just like she'd seen Sawyer do behind the maintenance shed at the resort. It had bought her an hour of relative peace and quiet as Zack practiced hitting a plastic golf ball into the circles. They were far larger than the holes that would be installed tonight, but the bigger targets helped Zack succeed, and that was worth any amount of dead grass.

It was as if she wasn't even here. On the one hand, it made getting the last of dinner ready sublimely easy. Fried chicken—Zack's favorite—had to be timed just right, and it was a luxury of sorts to be able to devote her full attention to the meal.

On the other hand, it rattled her to share Zack with someone else. Sawyer seemed to do something for Zack that she couldn't. Sure, she was grateful, but a corner of her heart was worried. Envious, even. She was his mother. She ought to be the one to reach him on such a level. Why was that chance afforded to Sawyer?

"You're right, this is amazing," Sawyer said to Zack later as he polished off a third piece of chicken.

"Is it better than Mom's coffee?"

Zack's nervy question made Molly's face heat up.

"Tough call," Sawyer replied. He gave Molly a quick look she couldn't discern. Zack seemed oblivious to the slight tension she could feel between her and Sawyer. Neither of them knew quite how to handle Zack's sudden and over-the-top response. Perhaps Mrs. Hollings had been right; all Zack really needed was just a tiny bit of success to turn the tide.

"Mr. Sawyer," Zack began, looking a bit serious.

"I think we can just go with Sawyer from here," Sawyer replied. He looked to Molly. "If that's okay with you."

Molly gave the reply she'd learned from her mother. "If Mr. Sawyer has invited you to call him Sawyer, you can do it. But only when a grown-up invites you."

Sawyer leaned toward Zack. "Good advice. Some grown-ups get picky about that sort of thing."

"Mrs. Binton would have a *cow* if I called her Biddy," Zack offered.

Molly's jaw practically hit the table. "Biddy is *not* Mrs. Binton's first name! And where did you learn a saying like that?"

"Danny Masters says it all the time."

"Sounds like Mrs. Masters has a whole herd of cows over her son's behavior," Sawyer said.

Zack broke into snickers of laughter, and even she couldn't suppress her own giggles. It struck her, just then, that Sawyer was actually laughing. A full-out, actual laugh—one that reached all the way to his eyes. It seemed to surprise him as much as it did her.

The bigger surprise was what a stunningly handsome man Sawyer was when he laughed.

"Sawyer," Zack said, still laughing, "I was trying to ask you something."

Sawyer traded his lighthearted face for a more serious one. "Sorry, buddy. I interrupted."

An unwelcome flash of memory shot into the moment. Steve, interrupting Zack at the dinner table. Repeatedly. Steve interrupting her, as well. It was something he'd always done. It seemed tiny at the time, but in hindsight it showed so much. She pushed the painful memory aside and returned to the present.

"After you put the holes in my yard, could you help me build my hippopotamus cart?"

Molly's pulse ground to a halt. She had no idea Zack was going to make such a request. He'd never done anything even close to the impulsiveness of that question. Usually such things required days of thought, hours of worry, endlessly hashing possible outcomes with her. *Oh, dear Lord*, her heart cried out. *What do we do with that?*

Stumped for any other tactic, Molly said, "That's an awfully big thing to ask, Zack. Sawyer hasn't even put in your golf holes yet, and he's a very busy man."

She needed to have a long conversation with Sawyer before he gave an answer to that request. And that was a conversation impossible to have right now. Was this a breakthrough for Zack, or was she watching her son throw himself into a sea of disappointment?

Sawyer seemed to think about it for a long time. *Be kind.* She shouted the mental message to the man across the table from her. *Please be kind.*

"You've thought about this?" Sawyer asked. It was a completely different question than "What on earth are you thinking?" which was the question clanging in Molly's brain at the moment.

Zack nodded. "Yep."

"I've never done it before. I could be lousy at it."

There was that word again. Molly tried to be grateful Sawyer was trying to let Zack down easy.

Zack got a look in his eyes that Molly could only describe as determined. Zack? Determined? It astonished her. "Or it could just be new."

Zack had tried to explain to her the meaning of *lousy* and *new* in the way he and Sawyer meant it. She understood part of it, but most of it eluded her because new was always exciting to her. Possibilities were wondrous things to her, not the enemies they seemed to be for Zack.

Whatever Zack was trying to say to Sawyer, whatever persuasion he was trying to make, Molly got the surprising feeling it was working.

"Kind of a risk, pulling me on board," Sawyer said, but there was little refusal in his tone.

"Yep. Figured that."

Molly looked back and forth between the man and boy and the conversation that went beyond her. *Stumped.* That was how she felt. *Utterly stumped.*

"Can I think about it?" He spoke to Zack like an equal. The simple respect in his words made Molly's throat tighten up. So many people wrote Zack off. Steve had abandoned any regard he'd ever held as the boy's father. But Sawyer took Zack seriously. *They are two serious people who understand each other's seriousness.* Molly couldn't think of any other way to describe what she was seeing.

"Sure," Zack said. There wasn't any disappointment in the fact that her son hadn't gotten a yes. In fact, he seemed—there wasn't another word for it—*pleased* that Sawyer was going to give it careful thought.

"Okay, then, what do you say we get those holes in?"

A quick collection of dirty dishes from the dinner table had the three of them standing in the backyard considering the layout of the Kane Family Three-Hole Golf Course.

"Tell me why you chose those spots," Sawyer said as he and Zack walked to each of the wobbly circles spray-painted on the lawn. He'd known—as she would have—that Zack didn't just spray circles willy-nilly. Her son had a detailed explanation for why he'd chosen each location.

The conversation went on for thirty minutes until Molly was swallowing the urge to shout, "Get on with it!" And yet Sawyer showed an endless patience for Zack's thoughts.

Finally, Zack walked back to stand beside her and point about the grass. "So we're gonna put them here, here and here." Only one of the spots was inside the circles he'd painted.

He'd changed plans. And he seemed remarkably calm about it. The doubt-filled, whirring gears she'd normally associate with him changing plans wasn't there. "Seems like good choices to me," she replied. Although she had no idea why they were good. Any spot on the grass looked as fine as any other to her.

Sawyer produced a small shovel and the plastic flowerpots out of the bag he'd brought, and got to work. It was a small job, but she couldn't help but admire his physical strength as he worked. Toned muscles showed when he pushed up the sleeves of his shirt to finish off the holes. If she looked past the darker parts of his personality, she supposed any woman would admire his physique. She'd never gone for the dark and brooding type, but then again, Steve hadn't done her much good as the complete opposite, had he? Steve's bright and blinding determination had left her and Zack in the dust. Maybe, if the dark could lighten up a bit, and brooding could soften up to mere thoughtful, there was hope for the man currently digging up her grass. After all, she'd seen something powerful in his eyes when he'd laughed at dinner.

Her thoughts were starting to head in dangerous directions. She was seeing unwise possibilities in the man. The pull she was starting to feel was dangerous. Molly told herself to stuff all such ideas away.

Until she heard the delightful *plunk* of a golf ball falling into the sunken flowerpot. And saw her son's smile. Then her mind went all kinds of unsafe places before she had any hope of catching it back.

Nine sets of sunken golf balls later, Sawyer piled his tools back into his bag, gave Zack a sedate little high five and said, "Yes."

"Yes what?" Zack questioned.

"Yes, I'll help you build your hippo cart." Molly's heart filled with a burst of sparkling light until he added, "But it might be lousy."

"I know," said Zack, returning Sawyer's gaze with one equally direct and serious. "I know."

## Chapter Seven

"People usually ride the carousel when they come in here, not stare at it."

Sawyer turned to find a man about his age wiping his hands on a red bandanna. He hadn't even seen the man working on the other side of the carousel.

"Then again, we're closed on Mondays, so I'm guessing you didn't come to ride. You strike me as long past the 'you gotta be this high to ride' age." He held a hand about as high as his waist.

"No," Sawyer said, a bit stunned the denial even needed to leave his lips. "Not here to ride."

"Wyatt," the man said, extending a now clean hand.

"Sawyer."

"I think I've seen you over at The Depot," Wyatt said. "I tend to get my coffee at the bakery, but when I need the high-octane stuff, The Depot's the way to go."

"I agree." Sawyer realized he ought to explain himself. "I saw the door open and I thought I'd better come get a good look at the hippo."

Wyatt narrowed his eyes at Sawyer until he connected the dots. "Oh, the parade thing. Your kid building a hippo?"

It felt odd to have people make that assumption about Zack. "Just helping out a friend." At that moment it struck him he didn't know if he meant Molly or Zack. Both, actually. When had he become friends with a second grader? "Zack Kane."

"Kane…" Wyatt looked off to one side as he tried to place the name. "Little guy. Kinda quiet." He held up a hand. "About this big. Wouldn't have pegged him for a hippo guy."

"It was a close call between that and the kangaroo," Sawyer offered.

Wyatt pointed at Sawyer. "Now, that I can believe."

A sudden, ridiculous jolt of worry shot through Sawyer that Zack had made the wrong choice. Wasn't he the one who staunchly assured Zack there was no wrong choice?

Wyatt stepped up on the carousel platform. "So you must know Molly."

"Yeah." There wasn't a simpler answer to a more complex fact in all of Colorado. "I'm teaching Zack to play golf." Why had that irrelevant fact jumped out of his mouth?

Surprise widened Wyatt's eyes. "You're that guy? You're the pro at Mountain Vista?" His question held no hint of admiration, but Sawyer was used to that.

"Far from it. I'm just the night security guy. But Molly asked me, and it's hard to say no to that woman." The fact that he was standing here considering carousel hippo construction was a testament to the truth of that statement.

Wyatt leaned his weight on the kangaroo. "Folks here aren't big fans of that place, but I expect you already know that."

"I get the general impression. Job's a job, right?" That was what he told himself every time he clocked in. Or every time someone stared too hard at his uniform shirt if he stopped at the market on his way home some mornings.

"If you're the kind of guy who can slough it off, sure. But you might want to look into a new line of work if you want to make friends in Wander."

He didn't want to make friends in Wander. He already had two more than he planned, and they were complicating his life enough as it was. It was time to change the subject. "So, building the hippo?"

"Easier than some, I expect. Big and square enough you could build it around almost anything. Not like the rooster or the seahorse. Those would be tougher to build." Wyatt got a glint in his eye. "Can you swipe a golf cart? You could build the biggest, baddest hippo Wander has ever seen if you could build it on a golf cart."

Sawyer wasn't ready to admit he had actually thought about it. "Maybe." He was actually calculating how to ask the grounds manager to lend him an out-of-service golf cart for two weeks, which told him his commitment to this idea had just ratcheted up to absurd.

Wyatt stood in front of the hippo and waved his hands around, visualizing. "If you sat the haunches over the wheels, and used the front end as the nose, it'd be amazing. Way better than the pair of flamingos I have to build using my girls' bicycles." He gave Sawyer a conspiratorial look. "Don't suppose I could talk you into a trade?"

Sawyer would admit he was growing fond of Zack. But enough to build a flamingo rather than a hippo? Not even for Molly. "Nope."

"I wouldn't, either, if I were you." Wyatt stepped down off the platform. "Nice thing you're doing there, helping the little guy out. His dad's not around much, is he?" He shrugged and offered, "My wife sings in the choir with Molly," by way of explanation.

"Not at all from what I can see." Molly seemed to sing with or to nearly everyone in Wander Canyon. So why on earth had she chosen *him* to help Zack? There had to be other people she knew better, ones more suited to the job. The unlikely choice she'd made in him followed him like a lost dog.

"Shouldn't be that way, should it?"

Again, a far too simple statement for a complex problem. "No."

"Well, then, it's a fine thing for you to step up. I'd be obliged to help in any way I can. I've had my fair share of Wander Canyon peering down their noses at me, so just give me a call if the Mountain Vistalanties get to you."

"The Vistalanties?" Like vigilantes? They actually had a name here for people opposed to the resort. Maybe he shouldn't use a golf cart. He and Zack might get pelted with rocks—or even golf balls—if they drove a decorated golf cart down Main Street as part of the anniversary parade.

"Probably should keep that little joke to myself. Folks here are nice, mostly. Narrow-minded, but most of 'em mean well. And no offense, but the resort deserves the reputation it's got. They haven't played nice."

"None taken." Sawyer gave his standard reply. "I just work there."

"If you want, I could keep an ear to the ground for a new job? I'm actually looking for a replacement for carousel repairman over here."

The world could not offer up a less suitable job for him than repairman for the Wander Canyon Carousel of Happiness. "You have no idea how unqualified I am for that."

"Oh, you'd be surprised," Wyatt said, nodding his head toward the little maintenance closet on the far wall. "Sure you don't want a ride? I'll turn it on for you if you'd like." He leaned in and whispered, "No one will ever know."

For a handful of seconds, Sawyer tried to visualize himself atop one of the animals, bobbing around the room while calliope music filled the air. The absurdity of it made him laugh. "I'll leave the riding to Zack."

"Your choice. But you strike me as a dragon kind of guy."

He had to ask. "Why do you say that?"

"All sharp teeth and hard scales on the outside, but I suspect soft and loyal on the inside. What other kind of guy researches a hippo for a little kid and his mom?"

"It's not like that," Sawyer said a little too quickly and with a bit too much emphasis.

Wyatt laughed and got the strangest look on his face. "Yeah," he said. "That's what I told myself at the beginning, too."

* * *

Molly glanced around at the faces of the other women in the Solos Bible study Tuesday night. They held nothing but compassion. Each of these women knew the particular struggles of raising a child alone. *I have no reason to think twice about sharing with them.*

And yet she did. It was ridiculous, prideful even, to hold herself back from the love she knew these women would offer. There'd be no judgment. That was what the prayer requests time of their meetings was about, wasn't it?

Tessa was leading this week—they all took turns—and Molly felt her calling on each woman around the circle like a tidal wave coming at her. She was so busy worrying about her own inability to hold it together that she wasn't even listening to the requests the other women were sharing. How awful was that?

The weekend had offered so much hope, but Monday had been absolutely awful. Today wasn't looking any better. Molly felt as if she was standing on a frozen lake, listening to the cracks in the ice travel toward her and waiting for the moment she went under.

"Molly?" Tessa's voice held an insistent concern. "You okay?"

It came out in a gush. An uncontrollable blurt of panic and frustration. "I-don't-know-if-I-can-do-it-anymore!" poured out of her along with a sudden bout of tears.

The women around the circle had every right to look surprised. She was supposed to be the sunny optimist, the Unsinkable Molly, as one of the older women in the choir was fond of saying after the old-time movie.

"I don't know what to do with Zack," she sobbed while accepting a tissue from the woman next to her. "I can't ever figure out what helps him. We take one step forward and then…" She didn't even have a word that didn't sound catastrophic. It wasn't—some part of her knew that—but it surely felt that way.

"What happened?" Tessa asked. "I thought you said Mrs. Hollings's golf idea was working out."

"It was." Was. The roller coaster of what worked and then didn't was the thing that made it so hard. "I got all excited for him. He has this connection with the guy who's teaching him. They seem to understand each other instantly. I'm jealous of that." The tears started up again. "I'm jealous of something good for my son because I can't seem to do it. What kind of mother does that make me?"

"An exhausted one," another woman chimed in with kindness in her eyes.

"Tell us what happened," Tessa repeated.

Molly told the story of the night Sawyer put the golf holes in their backyard. The new boldness—small, but definitely there—she saw in Zack's asking for Sawyer's help. The delight in his eyes when he sank that first putt. The "maybe we're on our way out of this" feeling that filled her heart when Sawyer agreed to help build the hippo.

"And then yesterday it all went away," she lamented to the group. "He got some directions mixed up on some homework and came home with a marked-up paper. Somebody said something at school, but he wouldn't tell me what it was. I just watched him start down that whole cycle of worry again. School, the carousel festival, you name it. And do you know what I did?"

No one replied, but she wasn't really asking the question anyway. "I told him to go outside and play with the golf holes. That was the new success, right? The thing that was working. I thought it would *help*." She practically moaned the last word.

"It didn't?" Tessa asked gently.

"It made it all so much worse," Molly cried. "He was too worked up. I didn't see that. He just kept missing and missing and getting angrier and angrier. I found him whacking one of the clubs against a rock, bending it all out of shape. Those aren't even his clubs." What was the point in stopping the tears now? It was all out there, raw and humiliating.

She'd thought about calling Sawyer last night. She couldn't admit to these women how close she'd come to doing it. Molly was desperate not to have to keep handling all this all alone. She'd wanted to share her frustration with the man who was starting to occupy way too many of her thoughts. She wanted him to look at her with the same loyal patience he looked at Zack.

It couldn't be healthy to lean on this unexpected, impossible-to-understand friendship—and she was going to keep using that word *friendship* because it was far too scary to think of it in any other terms.

What was growing between the three of them *was* scary. Sawyer was a virtual stranger. Good mothers didn't deliver their fragile sons into the hands of strangers. And wise women certainly didn't think about their sons' unofficial golf teachers in the ways she was trying not to think about Sawyer. Trying, and failing. The tangle of new thoughts and old fears had begun to choke her lately.

"Boys are a challenge," Grace Douglas said—and she spoke from experience. She'd never had to go fetch Zack from the Wander Canyon Police Department as many times as Grace had to with her son. *Yet.* "A boy like Zack? And all on your own, besides? I don't know how you do as well as you do."

"Not well at all." Molly cringed. Her wailing had taken over Solos, and that wasn't fair. Every woman in the room had struggles, not just her.

"That's not true." Tessa got up and crossed the room to sit next to Molly. "Zack has made progress. We all see it. You just can't see it now on account of last night's setback."

"Last night felt like way more than a setback. I spent today waiting for the phone to ring about what new school closet Zack has locked himself into." *I spent today trying not to call Sawyer, too.*

"But it didn't ring," Tessa said reassuringly. "Maybe learning to express his frustrations—granted in something resulting in less damaged sports equipment—will be a good thing for him."

"I'm glad you told us," another woman said. "We get it. You have to know that. We've all felt this way at one time or another."

"Or seven." A third woman managed a dark laugh and a shake of her head. "Last Thursday at our house was the stuff of nightmares."

"Now we know what to pray for."

"Do you?" Molly asked. "Because I sure don't."

"Peace in the storm," Grace offered. "It's all any of

us really need. Just the strength to get up and do it again tomorrow. And the day after."

Everyone seemed accepting of her outburst by the end of the meeting, but Molly's spirit still wobbled off balance.

Tessa caught up with her in the hallway. "Why didn't you call me?"

"What could you have done?" She was the one who ought to know how to help Zack, and any answer felt far out of reach.

"Calmed you down, maybe? Don't ever be afraid to share that kind of stuff, Molly. We've all been there. Every last one of us." She pulled Molly into a hug.

"I took over the meeting." It felt as if she owed an apology to each mother in the room.

"Because you needed to. Two weeks ago it was Linda, next week it could be me at my wit's end. No one needs you to be your usual bundle of happiness here. We do real life here, you know that. It's the only way any of us can keep our heads above water."

Tessa's reporter observational skills seemed to kick in, and she narrowed her eyes at Molly. "This is about more than Zack, isn't it?"

Molly didn't answer. Any denial she gave probably wouldn't stop Tessa anyway.

They walked a little farther down the hall before Tessa asked, "Did you call him?"

"No." It sounded so unconvincing that Molly felt compelled to admit, "I wanted to." Seeing no judgment on her friend's face, she went on. "It felt so good to see it all not fall on me. To watch Zack look to someone else. Part of me was grateful." She caught Tessa's eyes. "Part of me was jealous."

"It's nice to have someone pay attention to your son." Tessa's mouth turned up in a bit of a grin. "Maybe it's nice to have someone pay attention to you, too."

Molly stiffened up. "That night was about Zack."

"Only about Zack?"

"You should have seen it, Tessa. It was like watching Zack reach for who he could be. Zack actually asked Sawyer to help. Directly. No hemming and hawing or fidgeting. And his face when he got the ball in the hole the first time? I was floating around on a cloud of gratitude."

"Just gratitude? Maybe just a tiny bit of interest? He's not too hard on the eyes. And good with Zack? Helping him the way he is? Hard to beat that."

Molly shook her head. "You know I can't go there."

Tessa leaned back against the hallway wall. "Why not? You got a rough deal with Steve. The cancer's been gone two years. I like to think Zack deserves a truly happy mom, not one who just acts happy all the time."

Molly sighed and did her best to ignore the direction Tessa was leading the conversation. "I was so happy to see him happy. Thrilled to see him even a little bit confident. Yesterday's crash wiped all of that away."

"Hey, yesterday doesn't take any of that away. He got there once. That means he can get there again."

Molly wanted to believe that. She was just too tired and frustrated to hold it as truth. And, when she was truly honest, too frightened that Zack—and maybe even she—needed Sawyer to get him there.

"Make me a promise," Tessa said.

"What?"

"Tell yourself—tell your *heart*—it's okay to think about having new *friends*." Tessa put some emphasis on the final word, letting Molly know she meant a bit more than that. "It's what you tell Zack, isn't it?"

Molly frowned at her friend. "No fair using my own advice against me."

"Hey," said Tessa with a smile. "What are friends for?"

# *Chapter Eight*

Molly stood in the parking lot of the Mountain Vista Golf Resort the following morning while Zack was at school. She faced the little building she knew was Sawyer's security office, standing at the ready beside Sawyer's truck with a set of coffees again.

She'd asked for the morning off because he had to be told.

Not that spending a precious morning off getting this personal with Sawyer Bradshaw was an especially good idea, but it would prove to him why they had to be careful. It would ensure the distance between them she was coming to realize she'd need.

If she told him about what she'd been through, she could make him see why Zack's welfare had to come before everything else. Why these weren't ordinary golf lessons and the hippo cart wasn't an ordinary project. Yes, she was risking a highly personal conversation with someone she shouldn't get highly personal with, but Molly couldn't come up with another option. She had to have this conversation. Face to face. And this definitely wasn't one for the counter at The Depot. Or anywhere near Zack, for that matter.

*Stay beside me, Lord*, she prayed as she watched Sawyer exit the small building and wave goodbye to whomever was inside taking over for the day. *Give me the right words.*

He looked tired. No, weary. Tired was a temporary thing. Weary was a long, steep haul. It wasn't hard to recognize weary when you slogged through it yourself. Only she kept her weariness at bay with a determined cheerfulness.

Sawyer wore his on his sleeve, a hard shell to keep the whole world at a distance. The whole world, that is, except for Zack. *Does Sawyer realize Zack is cracking his way underneath that shell? Does he realize what a privilege—and a danger—that is?*

Surprise halted Sawyer's steps as he caught sight of her and the coffees waiting by his truck. He smiled before he could stop himself, and Molly tried not to let that wiggle its way inside her determination. Why did he have to have such a nice smile? And why did she have to notice he only gave that smile to her?

"What's this?" He looked around. "Did I forget we had a lesson?"

"No, that's Thursday after school."

Sawyer's eyes widened just a bit at the realization that she had come to see him. Molly pushed aside how pleased he seemed to be at that. "Can we talk?" She'd noticed a bench under a tree a little ways away and nodded her head in that direction. She tried to keep her tone light and casual, but failed miserably.

He caught it. "Everything okay? Has something happened to Zack?"

*You happened to Zack*, she thought. "Zack is… having a bit of a time." When Sawyer's worry doubled, she was quick to add, "Nothing you did, just… Zack being Zack." She sighed and passed him the coffee. "And me being me, I suppose."

"You worry a lot about him." He said it so tenderly. As if it were a virtue instead of a burden.

She cradled her own cup in her hands, grateful to have something other than Sawyer's gentle eyes to look at. "He gives me a lot to worry about. Which isn't helpful, because I don't want to model a worrisome heart to him." She stopped herself from going down that road. That wasn't why she was here.

Sawyer sat back against the bench. "I like him."

It seemed such an un-Sawyer-like thing to say that Molly's throat tightened up. So many people's affections for Zack seemed to come with qualifiers—*"He's a special boy." "He's misunderstood." "He sees the world differently."* To simply *like* him felt like such a gift. It made it far harder to resist the giver.

"He certainly likes you. Do you know what he told me the other night, after we put the golf holes in?"

She'd almost texted him, but the remark could be so misconstrued she'd opted to wait and tell him in person. But then Monday had happened, and it seemed pointless.

"What'd he say?"

"I hope you won't take this the wrong way, but he said you make him feel less like an oddball. He meant it as a compliment," she rushed to add.

Sawyer's eyes narrowed as he considered the back-handed compliment, then his face softened into another smile. "I'm glad, I guess."

She dove in. "We need to be careful. He's had a hard life and we need to be careful."

"I get things are hard for him. I think that's why..."

She cut him off and dove in all the way. "I had cancer."

Sawyer closed his jaw midword. The declaration hung in the air between them, raw and uncomfortable.

Molly took a deep breath and went on. "Just before Zack turned five I found a lump. It was malignant, and I went through surgery and radiation." The words felt hard and sharp, as if they scraped her chest as they came out. Still, it wasn't as bad as she had expected. She tried very hard to keep that part of her life tightly locked up in a little black box that hid behind her stalwart optimism. "Steve had already made his spectacular exit, so it was a very tough time for us. For him."

There was a long pause before Sawyer said, "That's rough."

"It was. I tried hard not to let it affect Zack, but of course that was impossible."

"Stuff like that changes you. Leaves scars, even when it comes out okay."

She knew, without him explaining at all, that personal experience had taught him that truth. Zack saw a reflection of his own scars in Sawyer's, even without knowing what Sawyer's scars were or how they got there.

He turned and looked at her for the first time in their

conversation. *Really* looked at her. Those eyes. It wasn't fair what his eyes did to her. "Are you okay?"

That was the million-dollar question, wasn't it? "Okay" had so many different definitions—which ones mattered most? The pull growing between them, the rebellious attraction she'd felt Saturday night made her want to shout, *I'm complicated!* in giant letters. Molly kept reminding herself there were so many reasons to keep a safe distance.

Molly stayed within the safety of the facts. "I've been cancer-free for two years. Signs are all good. But there's never any certainty in these things." She took a long sip of her coffee, needing to get her feet back underneath her after the blow of that admission. "You always worry."

"Does Zack worry?"

There were days where the weight of that question pressed her down. Where she felt her own body cursed Zack as much as it cursed her. In what world was it okay to give cancer to an overanxious little boy's mom? What higher purpose could God possibly have in that? Pastor Newton told her not to think that way, but on some sleepless nights it was impossible not to. "Of course he worries." Molly hated how close to tears those words brought her. "I'm all he's got."

"I don't think that's true." It wasn't placating, the way he said it. She was somehow sure Sawyer was stopping himself from saying, "He has me." His eyes looked like he had that thought. And yet, he of all people would respect the massive promise in those words.

It gave her the opening she needed to say what she came to say. "Zack doesn't depend on people. Life's taught him he can't. But for whatever reason, he's decided to depend on you."

Sawyer knew that. She could see the knowledge in the way he tightened his jaw. It sat hard on the man.

"I know you didn't ask for that. But he's connected with you." She clutched the coffee cup so hard it bent closer to an oval than a circle. "And while I'm trying hard to be glad for that—and I am, truly—" she looked as straight into his eyes as she dared "—you need to know how easily that could break him. How careful you need to be with him. With his trust. If you let him down, I…" Molly broke her stare and swallowed hard against the threat of tears.

"Molly." He said nothing but her name. But the way he said it said everything. If she'd had any doubt of how strong the pull was growing between them—a pull she knew she had to ignore—the tone of his voice and his eyes confirmed it. If anything, it told her that coming here, saying this and making sure he knew how precarious things were for her and Zack, had been the right choice.

"This has to be about Zack. I have to be sure you know that." She wouldn't come out and say, "It can't be about me," so she had to trust that her words got the message through. This would have been so much easier if there weren't volumes behind his eyes, if he didn't radiate that "lost but noble" soul vibe that always did her in.

"Zack is the most important thing here," he said. While the solemnity of his tone put her a bit at ease, it also implied Zack's needs weren't the *only* thing here. Was Sawyer's telling choice of wording a skilled response or simple truth? It didn't matter, as long as she came away from this conversation with the agreement that Zack was the most important thing. That would be worth admitting what she'd been through, admitting that the sunny optimism she showed the world didn't come easy. Letting him know they couldn't grow closer.

He looked out over the pristine grounds of the golf course. "Funny how life can slice itself in two parts. How everything becomes before or after."

"I'll have to let you know. I don't feel like I've gotten to 'after' yet. I'm still mucking through from checkup to checkup."

Sawyer shook his head slightly at the words. "Mucking through. Yeah." He was mucking through something of his own, that was obvious.

With anyone else, Molly would have asked him to tell her about it. She'd have found ways to be encouraging, to share how her faith and her friends helped so much to pull her through.

She couldn't do that with Sawyer. Knowing the thing that pressed on him—and it was huge, whatever it was—would bring them closer. And she didn't have a strong enough defense to keep that at bay. This had to be all about Zack.

He looked like he might be mustering up the courage to say more, so Molly squared her shoulders and looked at her watch. "I should let you go." Goodness, now whose choice of words was telling?

"Thanks for the coffee." The exchange felt absurdly mundane given the conversation they'd just had.

"See you tomorrow at The Depot."

She turned to leave until he called, "Molly," again.

For a second she wondered if she could pretend she hadn't heard him, but she was only few feet away. Molly had no choice but to turn and face him again.

"He's fortunate to have you. You're a good mom."

The sincere compliment dug into her, sharp and sweet at the same time. Why had he said the one thing sure to drag down her defenses? "I'm trying." *I'm trying hard. I pray you're a blessing to my son. The last thing Zack needs is more hurt.*

Sawyer spent the rest of the day trying to figure out what had compelled Molly to meet him like she did. It only took the next day's golf lesson to find out.

Zack was moody, dark and prickly. Which made for terrible golf, so of course things spun quickly downward. Sawyer cut the lesson short to head for the clubhouse in search of pen and paper. Today's time would be better spent making plans for the hippo cart than learning what irons and woods were for.

"Grumpy golf isn't worth playing," he said as they walked through the clubhouse snack bar. It was crowded and noisy, so Sawyer led them through the building to camp out on the floor of the small banquet hall that sat at the far end.

While it wasn't an especially big room, Zack surprised Sawyer by opting to sit under the room's grand piano. An odd choice of fort, granted, but Sawyer decided to play along and get down in between the instrument's three ornately carved legs beside Zack.

"Got any ideas for your hippo?" he said, trying to sound cheerful. It felt goofy.

Zack just shook his head.

"I got some from Mr. Walker, the guy who runs the carousel. Want me to show you?"

Zack gave him a nod. A pouty nod, sure, but a nod.

Sawyer took the paper and sketched out an idea built on what Wyatt Walker had told him. "What do you think?"

"'S okay." It lacked a certain enthusiasm. Sawyer found himself disappointed, but it wasn't surprising given the boy's dark mood.

"Why do I get the feeling you're not going to like any idea right now?"

Zack said nothing, but pulled his knees up to his chin and wrapped his arms over his shins. He might as well have rolled himself up in a little ball like an armadillo. Did they have one of those on the carousel?

He knew that feeling. If you got too far into that dark spiral, it was hard to climb back out. You certainly couldn't talk your way out of it. No one could suggest you out of it—although he was certain Molly would try. For a rebellious moment, Sawyer imagined how Molly would look and what she would say to him if she were beside him in one of his darker moments. He liked the image. Too much.

Shaking the warmth of that idea aside, Sawyer looked over his head at the underside of the piano. He knew what Molly would say about where he was right now. She would call this one of her "God things." She'd see no coincidence in the fact that he was currently hunched under the very thing he used to use to pull him out of his dark moods. Up until recently, the piano had always been the coping mechanism to help him crawl back out of a funk.

Why had he stopped playing altogether after the vehicle crash? He couldn't really explain it. Maybe he was punishing himself, denying himself the pleasure of music as penance for sending that car into the corner of that building and ending those innocent lives. Talent was for worthy people. And he hadn't felt worthy in months.

Maybe because it was for Zack and not for him. Maybe that was what enabled him to crawl out from under the piano whether or not Zack followed him. If he couldn't bring Zack to the rescue, the rescue would come to him.

It felt ridiculous and shocking to sit down on the piano bench. Sawyer had the sensation of trespassing as he lifted the long shiny black cover off the keyboard. Part of him was afraid to touch the keys, to let his hands settle on them for fear they wouldn't remember how.

Instead, it came flooding back to him, and his foot found the pedal below without even thinking. Sawyer waited for the choice of music to slip out of his fingers, falling into place for a piece even before his conscious mind chose which song to play.

Could he, still? Had his gift been stripped away like all the other joys in his life? The prospect of it all coming back to him was just as frightening as discovering it was gone.

Sawyer closed his eyes, imagining the little ball of a boy hiding under the piano. Something low and soft. By instinct his fingers moved into the opening notes of a Joplin number called "Solace." They hung soft and slow in the air at first, then began to tumble into higher notes in a minor key, picking up a little bit of momentum before hanging on cliffs of pauses and tumbling back down into the lower tones.

He couldn't see Zack, of course, but he could feel the boy's surprise. "Solace" started out as a sad-happy ragtime song that nobody knew, then turned into a happy-sad song many people recognized.

He messed up at least half a dozen measures, his memory stalling on a few parts so that the rhythm wasn't anything close to consistent. The song sounded the way he knew Zack felt. Maybe even the way Sawyer felt, for his chest felt like a dusty old trunk someone had just pulled open.

Sawyer didn't dare stop, and he didn't dare look down. He moved on through the song, hoping no one would come into the banquet hall at the sound of his extremely mediocre playing.

At the end of the song, Sawyer caught sight of Zack's small blue sneakers coming into view out from underneath the piano. The armadillo had unrolled himself a tiny bit.

Emboldened, Sawyer let only a small silence fall between the end of "Solace" and the low notes that started the "Magnetic Rag." He hit one of the lowest notes with an oversize emphasis, probably booming right over Zack's head, and was rewarded with the smallest of giggles.

By the end of the number, Zack was out from underneath the piano and gaping at him. Wide, stunned eyes stared at Sawyer from the floor. By the end of the "Pine Apple Rag," Zack was perching his elbows on the end of the piano bench and staring, amazed, at Sawyer. By the time Sawyer started the "Maple Leaf Rag"—one almost everyone recognized—Zack was sitting on the piano bench next to him.

Without thinking about it, Sawyer leaned playfully into Zack as he made a show of reaching across the boy for the high notes. Zack laughed, and Sawyer could barely believe he felt the same bubbling up out of his own chest. He missed note after note on the travels up and down the keyboard, and didn't care. The perfection of the piece didn't matter at all. What mattered was that he could still do it. He could still crawl into the complexities of ragtime piano, could still pull the cascades of notes out from his fingers.

It hadn't gone away. The music met him where he was—as it had always done—and took him away from the darker places. And he had shared that with Zack. *I may not be worthy*, he told himself as he caught Zack's eye with a particularly silly trill of high notes, *but I'm useful*.

He used to feel so useful. Important and necessary, a protector of a community. He'd become useless, allowed himself to be declared "no longer useful." None of that had really changed, except that this moment took just a tiny bit of the old Sawyer back.

He finished the number and let the final notes hang in the air. The importance of the moment—for reasons he couldn't hope to explain—pounded against his chest.

"Whoa!" Zack's eyes were still wide.

It fit. "Whoa, indeed," Sawyer agreed.

"You play the piano."

There was something amazing about Zack's use of the present tense. *I play the piano*. Not *I used to play*.

Sawyer found himself staring at his hands as if he had just been reintroduced to an ancient friend.

"Play something else," Zack pleaded.

"Happy or sad?" It was a fair question. The best music matched your current mood. And he was rather curious which Zack would pick now.

"Silly," Zack replied after a moment of face-scrunching consideration.

Sawyer cast back into his near-encyclopedic memory of ragtime piano tunes. "Dill pickles or frog legs?"

"What?" Zack burst out laughing.

"Choose. Dill pickles or frog legs?"

It wasn't hard to guess which a seven-year-old boy would choose. "Frog legs!"

Sawyer felt a smile creep the whole way up from his feet as he launched into "Frog Legs Rag." In a moment of inspiration, he had Zack crawl onto his lap and place his hands on top of his as they danced across the keyboard.

It was the closest thing to joy he could remember feeling.

"Do the pickle one!" Zack implored. The look in the boy's eyes as he craned his neck back to look at Sawyer just about sliced Sawyer's heart in half. The small heft of Zack's head against his shoulder weighed everything and nothing at all.

They laughed through "Dill Pickle Rag" and two more before the banquet room door opened and a shocked Molly stared as if the whole world had turned upside down.

# Chapter Nine

Molly put an artful dollop of foam on a chai latte and looked at the clock again Friday morning. Sawyer would be here in ten minutes, and she still hadn't found a way to talk to him about what had happened.

Mostly because she didn't really know what *had* happened. On the surface, Sawyer had played some music for Zack when he was in his funk. But those actions didn't come close to explaining what had truly happened. Sawyer had found a way to reach through to Zack on his downward spiral and turn it around before it took him under.

And she couldn't argue that it was just any music. Creature of melody that she was, she played music in the house all the time, but it never had that profound an effect on Zack as she had seen in that golf course banquet room. Somehow, Sawyer's music had reached Zack in a way she couldn't.

Was it the music? Or the man?

Either way, she couldn't come up with the words for what a victory that was. Whatever she said in thanks wouldn't be enough. She'd said thanks—dozens of times—the other day, but more needed to be said.

When Sawyer walked through the door ten minutes later, Molly realized something else. Sawyer had changed, too. Not dramatically, but his bearing was a little bit lighter. The lines of his face weren't so tightly drawn. He looked more at home in the world. The extraordinary connection between him and Zack healed both boy *and* man. How was she supposed to keep her distance from a powerful truth like that?

Molly started with something simple. "Zack put your drawings up on the refrigerator. And he asked me to take him to the hardware store after school to choose the right gray color paint for his hippo. He's excited."

"That's great," Sawyer replied.

"No, you don't get it. Zack's *excited*. That's so much more than great." She began making the espresso needed for Sawyer's Americano. She didn't have it ready and waiting this time because she wanted to add to the time they spent talking. And the truth was, his visits were becoming the highlight of her mornings.

"It's amazing," she went on. "I was worried he'd pull the plug on the whole thing the way he was upset."

"Did you ever figure out what set him off?"

What set Zack off? Some days Molly felt as if she'd be spending the rest of her life trying to figure out what set Zack off. "No. I'm not even sure it matters. The list of things that get under his skin is a mile long. And I feel like it changes every day."

"That has to be rough." She couldn't stop herself from noticing every little thing about the man. The way his hair kicked up into a little bit of a wave at the ends.

The way the sun would occasionally catch the gold in his eyes and set them off like firelight. The scuffs on the leather of his watchband. The scar that ran from the back of his jaw down one side of his neck. The way he held her eyes for just a second longer than usual this morning.

"But he pulled himself out of it," she continued. "Or you pulled him out of it. That's huge. How did you know what to do?"

She must have tried a dozen different types of music to help pull Zack from one of his glum moods. It had never worked. And ragtime? Never in a million years would she have associated that cheery, old-time music with the man in front of her.

Sawyer shrugged. "I didn't know what to do. To tell you the truth, I hadn't touched a piano in months before that moment. If he hadn't crawled under the piano, I never would have thought to try it."

Zack hadn't mentioned that. "He hid under the piano?" The instant vision of Zack cowered under that massive grand piano sent a sharp sting through her heart.

"More like seeking shelter. I think the room felt too big for him. If he was hiding, he wouldn't have liked me crawling down under there with him."

Molly tried not to gape. "You crawled under the piano with him?" Sawyer wasn't a small man. The image of him crouched under there with little Zack would have made her laugh if it hadn't been so heartwarming. In fact, that persistent glow in her heart—the one she was trying hard to ignore—doubled at the image.

"He fit under there a lot easier than me, that's for

sure." The corner of his mouth turned up—quickly and easily this time. She relished the idea of being able to bring a smile out of him. And what a smile it was.

Molly had to tell herself to stop staring and snap a lid onto his coffee. But the minute she slid it across the counter, her eyes found his again. The small skip in her heart had nothing to do with caffeine.

"He had me download twelve different ragtime songs onto his tablet last night," she told Sawyer. "He played them for hours."

"Kid's got good taste." Sawyer picked up the coffee, but didn't turn to leave. He lingered. She liked that.

"So," he began, a bit sheepishly, "I've got a request of sorts."

After this past victory, Molly couldn't think of a request she would refuse this man. "Sure."

"How much free garage space do you have at your house?"

"It's a one-car garage, but I can park my car outside for a while to make room. For the festival cart?" They had made plans for Sawyer to come over and begin actively building the cart the next evening.

"Yeah, with the way weather changes around here, I don't think we should build it outside. But also…well, it's a bit of a surprise. I'll bring it with me tomorrow afternoon. I just wanted to make sure you had room for us to get started. Make sure Zack is wearing clothes that can get messy." He froze for a moment. "Zack will be okay getting messy, won't he?"

Molly had thought about that herself. Some messes he was fine with; other kinds of mess threw him for a loop. "We'll have to figure that out as we go along, I suppose." She felt the need to say it again. "Thank you. For understanding him. For understanding both of us."

She regretted that last statement right away. The attraction growing between them made it way too easy to slip up and say things that should be left unsaid. She'd made it clear this was to be about Zack, and she trusted Sawyer to honor that.

"I like the little guy." The tilt of Sawyer's head spoke of such an honest affection that Molly's heart skipped a little. A lot, actually.

For a moment the air felt thick and close between them. Molly was both glad and disappointed there was no one else in the shop. Even the full length of the train car seemed too small a space to be alone with Sawyer Bradshaw this morning. It made her wonder if tomorrow night was going to be fun or challenging. Likely both.

Sawyer cleared his throat and tipped his coffee at her. "Just make sure there's space in the garage, and that I can get up the drive. Lots to unload. And don't say anything to Zack. I want this to be a surprise."

"Be prepared for anything," Molly advised. "Surprises aren't always the best way to go with Zack." When she saw Sawyer's features fall, however, she added, "But somehow, I figure this one is worth risking."

The smile returned to his face. Molly would pray hard that the surprise went well. All three of them could sure use the boost.

"Mom! Mom!" Zack raced into the kitchen the following afternoon with eyes as big as saucers. He grabbed her arm right out of the dishwater, sending a splash of suds over Molly's leg and the floor. "You gotta come look!"

If it was Sawyer and his surprise, he was ten minutes early. "What is it?"

"A great big truck just pulled into our driveway."

Molly shot up a quick prayer of thanks that Zack looked excited rather than upset. She wiped her free hand on her jeans as Zack yanked her around the corner to the front room window. Just as Zack had described, a large white truck with green lettering was backing into her drive, the incessant beep of a reverse gear announcing its arrival.

Molly had to look at it twice, and almost shake her head in disbelief, to register the sight.

A flatbed truck bearing the Mountain Vista logo was backing up her driveway. On the bed, tied down and covered with a clear tarp, was a golf cart.

She opened the front door as the beeping stopped and the truck stilled. Sawyer climbed down out of the driver's seat. There was no other word for it: he was grinning. Not the careful, tentative smile he occasionally offered. This one lit up his face in a way that made her breath hitch.

"Whoa!" Zack gasped beside her. "It's one of the baby cars from the golf course!"

Molly and Sawyer both laughed. "That's one way to put it," Sawyer said as he hoisted himself up onto the truck bed and began to undo the belts and tarp. "This one was headed for the junk heap so I got permission to put it to a better use."

"You mean it doesn't work?" Alarm pitched Zack's voice up.

"Not great, but we can fix it to do what we need. Say hello to your hippo, Zack."

"No way!" Zack's hands went to his head as if it were going to explode. In a good way.

"You've got to be kidding me. This is the surprise?" Molly had been thinking it was a wheelbarrow or a big wagon or something—but a golf cart? This was so far beyond what she'd expected. The grand and generous gesture nearly brought her to tears.

Sawyer hit a few switches on a control and the truck bed began to tilt like a tow truck. Even the neighbor across the street came out their front door to see the unusual delivery. If anyone was going to put up a fuss about a Mountain Vista truck in her driveway, Molly couldn't bring herself to care. Not after this.

"I told you Mr. Walker suggested we could soup up a golf cart to make the perfect hippo," Sawyer explained.

"Well, yes, I saw the drawings Zack brought home." They'd actually been quite clever. "But I didn't think you'd really…"

Sawyer pulled a pair of gloves from his back pocket. "Yeah, well, to tell you the truth, neither did I." At that moment, he seemed just as baffled by his enthusiasm as Molly was. If God was in the surprise business as much as Pastor Newton said, He certainly was proving it today.

Molly helped Sawyer and Zack go through the mechanics of backing the cart down off the truck. She watched them work together pushing it into the space she'd cleared in the garage. The whole time she grasped for words to say how grateful she was, how this huge gesture touched her deeply.

A sharp note hid under all the gratitude, however. She couldn't help thinking that it should be Steve doing this. It seemed like such a father-and-son project—she'd almost opted out of participating just because it would shine a spotlight on the hole Steve had left in Zack's life.

A hole Sawyer was now filling. But for how long? She'd never gotten the sense that he was in Wander Canyon to stay. He wasn't trying to fit into the community—just the opposite most days. What would it do to Zack if he connected so deeply to Sawyer and then Sawyer left? *He can't have another man abandon him, Lord*, she prayed as Zack dashed back into the house to get the drawings Sawyer had given him. *Don't You dare let that happen.*

Molly took advantage of the quick moment alone with Sawyer. "This is…amazing. Thank you for caring so much." Even as the words left her mouth, they seemed too personal.

Sawyer's face flushed a bit. "I know it's a bit over-the-top. And I'll make sure things don't get out of hand."

Was he talking about the project, or how close he was getting to Zack? To her? She didn't dare ask.

"Can you get it done? There's only a week until the festival." The short timetable meant Sawyer would be around her house a lot over the next seven days. She found that prospect dangerously appealing.

"It's mostly just paint." Sawyer ran a hand over a dent in the cart's fender. "We have to sand it to get the paint to stick on the finish, but once that's done it should go pretty quick." He gave her an apologetic look.

"Although I can't vouch for the artistry—it might only barely look like a hippo with my skills."

She'd been wondering what her role in all this would be. "I'll be glad to help with that."

"Mom's good at drawing," Zack chimed in as he came back with the papers. "What do we do first?"

Molly practically gasped. Usually Zack had to think about a project for hours—even days—before starting. He had to "worry it through" before he could commit to starting something. And yet he looked absolutely ready to dive in this minute.

"Oh, wait. I forgot." Zack turned back toward the house.

Sawyer looked at Molly with a raised eyebrow. "What'd he forget?"

"Your guess is as good as mine. Is it okay for him to be sanding this? Isn't it fiberglass?"

"Mostly plastic," Sawyer replied, turning to fetch a canvas workbag from the truck. "But yes, I thought of that." He reached into the bag and produced three sets of safety goggles and dust masks, along with packets of sanding block and papers. "It'll still be messy, but totally safe. I checked with Wyatt since he knows about auto bodywork and the carousel, just to be sure."

He'd made sure it was all safe—there wasn't a faster way to a mother's heart. The cliché phrase struck a little too close to home. Sawyer was finding his way to her heart, and she wasn't sure she could stop it. Or if she even wanted to. "Thank you for that." Again, the lack of sufficient words tied her tongue in knots. "Thanks for all of this."

"Don't thank me yet. I'm way out on a limb here."

She knew that. Sawyer was putting himself way out

there for Zack's sake. Molly's heart grabbed on to that truth and held it close. She was losing the battle to keep her distance, she could tell.

The sound of ragtime piano filled the garage as Zack came back with his computer tablet and a little speaker. "Now we got music to help us work."

"Great idea, Zack." Sawyer held out the pint-size mask and goggles. "Ready to get messy?"

Zack's enthusiastic nod felt large enough to fill the entire canyon.

Sawyer blew the dust off the cart's back fender and stretched his back. He was going to have to go to work in a few hours, and for the first time in forever he didn't welcome the idea. The appeal of the dark solitude had nothing on the welcome warmth of the afternoon he'd spent in Molly's garage. In Molly's presence.

He glanced over at Zack. The boy's brows were furrowed in focus behind safety goggles and a mask. His hands—inside the child-sized work gloves Sawyer had bought at the hardware store along with the other supplies—worked the sanding block back and forth.

What he'd said to Molly was true: he liked Zack. Sure, the boy was complicated and fearful, but Sawyer understood those feelings. He understood what it did to you to be certain the world wasn't your friend. It took a lot of energy to move through the world without Molly's nonstop optimism.

He stole a glance over at Molly. He'd been stealing them all afternoon and hoped she hadn't noticed. She had her hair wrapped up in some brightly colored bandanna. Her eyes were wide and sparkling and totally adorable behind the goggles and mask. The three of them had gotten into a miniature water fight washing down the cart, and it was the most playful he'd been in what…months? Years?

He was covered in dust, his shoulders ached, he'd cheated himself out of too much sleep to get this all done for tonight…and he didn't care. The sense of feeling useful again, of putting something right in the world instead of being a walking source of wrong, felt like new air in his lungs.

He could stay here all day. Near her, near Zack, reveling in the feelings that showed up in a chest that had been cold and empty for so long. He was starting to entertain ideas that defied Molly's request for distance. Reluctantly, he wiped the dust off his watch and pulled off the mask. "We ought to call it a day, don't you think?"

"Aww…" The look of disappointment that crossed Zack's face tucked itself away in a corner of Sawyer's heart.

Molly pulled off the gear and her bandanna. Her hair was still wet where Zack had gotten her with the hose, and it hung in delicate little ringlets around her cheeks and temples. She gave Zack a motherly look. "You definitely need a shower before bed. Maybe two."

"Maybe you can just hose him down in the driveway," Sawyer teased. Teasing? Now he was teasing?

"Noooo!" Zack yelped even as he grinned. He set down his mask and goggles, mussing his hair with both hands so that it stuck up in all directions. *Adorable* wasn't a word that came to his mind often, but it had stuck in his thoughts most of the night.

"Are you coming back tomorrow?" Zack asked eagerly.

"I'll come by after church if it's okay with your mom," Sawyer said. Molly's earlier conversation had warned him he needed to be careful about overstepping.

She nodded. "Our hippo's on a deadline."

She'd said *our.* Sawyer had to admit he liked that word a lot.

# Chapter Ten

A grown man should not feel this way.

The week had flown by and it was festival day. A parade of carts was about to start down Main Street. Sawyer was grinning like a fool and practically fidgety with anticipation.

Him. Fidgety with anticipation. Sawyer had stopped trying to explain the new version of himself showing up over the past week. Time with Molly and Zack had changed him. In ways he was nowhere near ready to admit or even welcome.

Sawyer lost any hope of controlling the ridiculous surge of pride that overtook him as he watched Molly maneuver the golf-cart hippo into line at the top of Main Street. Nor could he tamp down the glow under his ribs at Zack's mile-wide grin as he sat beside Molly in the cart. Or the elation at Molly's delighted face, knowing he had helped to put that joy there.

Wyatt Walker walked up beside him and gave an appreciative nod. "Outstanding job there, Bradshaw. I think Zack will take first prize."

Sawyer hadn't dared to hope for that. "Molly's just happy he actually took part."

"I didn't do half as well with the girls' bikes." He gestured to the wildly swaying heads of two flamingos somehow built on the bicycles of his twin stepdaughters.

"Oh, I don't know. Pretty clever stuff there." The girls were wearing pink sweat suits with some sort of black paper cone fitted like a curved flamingo beak to the front of their pink bicycle helmets.

Wyatt shook his head. "You're showing me up, and I'm supposed to be the Carousel Man."

Sawyer had to admit Walker's bit-of-a-renegade appearance and his cutting wit didn't exactly line up with the kind of carnival barker who would run a Carousel of Happiness. Lots of people in Wander Canyon weren't quite what they seemed on first pass.

Then again, that could cut both ways. After all, he was more than he seemed, wasn't he? There had been a lot of television footage of the squad car crash and the funeral of that mom and her boys. There was no escaping the inevitable: someone would connect the dots any day now, and he'd have to move on.

Trouble was, he was growing to like it here. He'd never planned on that happening. But he'd never planned anything that Molly Kane thrust into his life.

"You gave me the idea. It's just a paint job, and mostly of Molly's design at that."

"Anyone give you grief that it's a Mountain Vista golf cart?"

Sawyer had, in fact, been expecting someone to call him on that. Especially if Zack won some sort of prize. But it hadn't happened…yet. "Not so far."

"Well, steer clear of Norma Binton and maybe you'll get away clean." Wyatt pointed to a sour-looking old woman standing on the other side of the street. "Town grump. And the town gossip, which is a bad combination."

What would Norma Binton do if she got wind of Sawyer's role in that tragic accident? She'd be like all the others, not caring that the high-speed chase had been caused by a gang member. Giving no thought to how hard Sawyer had tried to avoid the crash, to how those final moments in his squad car played in his head all the time. People like Norma didn't care that his mind constructed dozens of tiny split-second decisions he could have made differently. The regrets that hounded him. If he'd just angled the car a hair to the left. If his reaction time had been half a second faster. If he'd called it into dispatch instead. If, if, if—he spent his days running ahead of a constant avalanche of ifs.

Sawyer made a mental note to avoid Norma Binton at all costs.

"Hey, look, they're starting." Wyatt pointed to a stout-looking man in a red top hat at the front of the line of carts. "That's Paul Redding. He was the perfect choice for grand marshal."

"Like the store?" Redding's General Store was just across the street. It was a gifty kind of shop—throw pillows and mason jars in the windows and not the sort of thing he ever ventured into. Molly, however, talked about it often.

"Paul ran it before his daughter Toni took it over. It's sort of a Wander Canyon thing to head over there and pick out a little treat or toy or whatever after riding the carousel, so the connection is perfect." Without his permission, Sawyer's mind crafted the image of him walking Zack over there after a carousel ride. With Zack's small hand in one of his and maybe even Molly's hand in... *Stop that*, he told his imagination. *That's not for you.*

"What about those people?" Sawyer broke his thoughts by pointing to the handful of people walking behind Paul. Each had a bright red ribbon sash across their chest. "Who are they?"

"The original carousel committee—or what's left of it. They helped build the thing way back when one guy had the idea to create the carousel. He'd seen too much tragedy in the war and decided to make a big dose of happiness. He passed on a few years back, but I like to think he left a pretty amazing legacy."

"I'll say." Sawyer had been so focused on disappearing, the thought of leaving any kind of happy legacy behind seemed downright impossible. Except for maybe today. Today he felt like he'd put just a little bit of good into the world. Into Zack and Molly's world, if nothing else.

The trill of a whistle sailed across the air, and Paul Redding positively beamed as he hoisted some sort of crazy baton someone had made for him. As he started off down Main Street, the crowd erupted in a cheer. Sawyer felt himself cheering right alongside Walker and everyone else. A thin layer of the hard shell he'd built up around himself seemed to peel off despite every effort to hold it in place.

Walker stayed beside Sawyer for the parade, giving

his own commentary on the carts as they went past. "Not bad, brother!" Wyatt called out as the man Sawyer recognized as Chaz Walker and his wife, Yvonne, pushed their little boy, Henry, in a wagon done up as a goldfish. Yvonne was blowing bubbles for a special effect. Chaz looked rather embarrassed to be parading his son in the event, but Yvonne was having a ball and Henry seemed to be having fun.

Wyatt snapped a photo of the young family. "I can whip this photo out anytime Chaz gets too serious. Which is a lot."

"This one was a no-brainer," Wyatt said as he pointed to a boy riding a cleverly designed turtle. "You had to figure Jake would rig up some kind of turtle for Cole." Based on the pumping of the young boy's body, Sawyer suspected a pedal-powered toy car was under the wide green kiddie pool that had been transformed into a turtle shell. He wore what looked to be a bicycle helmet painted green with half-white circles—baseballs?—painted to look like turtle eyes. It was a pretty impressive effort.

"I think I met his dad in the hardware store," Sawyer said.

"You'll get to know everyone in town eventually," Wyatt replied. "That's the beauty—and the pain—of Wander. No place to hide in this town."

Sawyer forced out a false laugh as the comment raced icily down his back. Wasn't that exactly why he was here? Had he made the wrong choice in coming out here? Should he have gone to some other big city rather than flee out to the mountains?

The thought warred with Molly's constant proclamations of him as some kind of answer to prayer, as if he was supposed to be exactly here. As if God had led him here. That couldn't be. He just didn't see himself as being worthy of that kind of attention from the Almighty.

"And there's the cart of the hour," Wyatt said as Molly and Zack drove slowly by. Cheers rose up as Zack waved. You could have lit the entire town up for weeks on the wattage of Molly's smile. Even from this distance, her eyes beamed like bright blue stars. When Zack's eyes found Sawyer, the joy in them shot through Sawyer like the jolt of a thousand coffees.

"Suppose so," Sawyer said, his throat unexpectedly thick. Looking at those two, at the rickety old golf cart that had now become a—yes, he'd admit it—pretty impressive hippopotamus, it wasn't that hard to think he'd done some good here. Maybe not God-ordained, answer-to-prayer good, but a happy accident. A small positive to push back against all the regret and sorrow of the past year. "Turned out okay."

"More than okay. I mean, the cart's awesome, but I gotta say, I don't think I've ever seen Zack Kane that happy. He always strikes me as such a serious kid. Somebody that young shouldn't be such a bundle of worries, you know?"

Wyatt meant no harm in the comment, but in the moment Sawyer understood a little of how Molly described the effect he'd had on Zack. People seemed to see Zack in terms of what he ought to be, or what he shouldn't be. Sawyer liked him for who he was. Liked him a lot for who he was.

Sawyer liked his mother—very much, too much—a lot, as well.

He knew Molly had been very clear about the limits of their relationship—if you could even call it that. Still, none of those logical warnings changed the constant pull he'd felt strengthening toward her all week. She was vibrant and beautiful as she drove the golf cart down the street at this moment, but she was *always* vibrant and beautiful. Even tired and worried, she was beautiful.

Life just radiated out of her, while he could only feel life seeping out of him. *Draining* out of him. Just being around her stemmed the tide of all the dark stuff. He'd spent so much delightful time around her getting this cart ready that next week terrified him.

Next week he'd have no real excuse to spend so much time around her. He was coming to need that time, to crave it. Would all the darkness swirl back up around him without Molly to hold it back? They were in a perfect bubble—enough time to enjoy her company and marvel at her impossibly buoyant spirit, but not enough time for her to figure out who he was and what he'd done.

That was the thing about bubbles. They eventually burst

To anyone else, Molly suspected this was just a simple, small-town festival. A bunch of people doing something creative and crazy to celebrate the pride Wander Canyon had in its carousel. And the carousel was worth celebrating. It was charming and whimsical and a little offbeat…just like Wander Canyon.

To Molly, today was a gigantic victory. A foothold, a

source of hope, an accomplishment and a golden memory all wrapped up in one goofy gray hippo cart.

She steered the lumbering little cart slowly down Main Street with all the grandeur of a New York City ticker-tape parade. She waved to friends and neighbors as if she'd been crowned Queen of Everything. She watched Zack smile and wave as if his introverted self had somehow fallen away with all that sanding.

For a shining half an hour, Molly watched her son triumph. What a gift that was. *What a blessing, Lord. Thank You.*

Sure, there were a few sideways glances at the use of a golf cart. No one in Wander Canyon owned one, so she could almost watch a few bystanders figure out that it must have come from Mountain Vista. Norma Binton scowled, but then again, Norma Binton scowled at everything. Some defiant part of her was glad to have played a role in redeeming the resort for the town. Not everything was ever one hundred percent bad. She'd held fast to her belief that there was a sliver of good in even the worst of people, that rainbows always hid inside storms if you kept looking long enough.

This hippo may be an ordinary gray, but he was every color of the rainbow in Molly's eyes.

And in someone else's eyes.

She scanned the length of the sidewalk until she saw Sawyer. He stood next to Wyatt Walker, then stopped talking with Wyatt to wave with uncharacteristic enthusiasm when he caught sight of Zack. Her whole body registered the moment her gaze locked with his. A powerful zing of gratitude, connection…and yes, affection surged through her.

She was coming to care for him. Quite a bit, despite the mountain of questions he raised in her. His connection with Zack meant the world to her, but Molly was running out of ways to tamp down the connection she herself felt to Sawyer. He was loyal. He knew how to care, but was trying hard not to. He was wounded, although she didn't yet know how or when.

"Broken people can recognize broken people," Mom had said. That was back in the final days of her mother's own battle with breast cancer, as everyone was wrapping their sore spirits around the understanding that this story wasn't going to have a happy ending. "How do I keep going?" she'd wailed at her mother's bedside. Losing Mom felt as if it would break her life in ways that couldn't be repaired.

Through her own damage—the failed marriage and the cancer—Molly had come to realize the truth of her mother's statement. Brokenness *was* a gift of sorts. It gave a rare and particular empathy you couldn't get any other way. A sense for the brokenness in others. Molly didn't know it then, but losing Mom at nineteen had given her the empathy it took to raise a boy like Zack.

It gave her the empathy to see so much in Sawyer's eyes. To feel such a powerful pull by what she saw there.

"Mom… *Mom!*" Zack was poking her arm even as they passed Sawyer and turned the corner to the parking lot in front of The Depot and the carousel, where all the carts were lining up at the end of the parade.

"What?" Molly was embarrassed she'd let her thoughts stray so much while at the wheel of a vehicle. A slow golf cart, but a vehicle nonetheless.

"Can you take my picture behind the wheel when we're parked? Can I pretend like I'm driving it?"

Not while the cart was moving, of course, but parked? What was the harm in a shot of him behind the wheel? It was a day worth remembering. She'd find a special frame and put the photo up on his bureau to remind him how new things could turn out wonderful. "Sure. But only after we're parked."

Molly carefully backed the cart into its assigned spot, face out so that the judges could award prizes later today. Zack slid gleefully behind the wheel, eyes wide and smile even wider. She snapped a few shots of him as he pretended to drive.

"Let's get a video, too," Molly suggested. She tapped the icon to switch her phone to the necessary mode.

The sound of the golf cart's horn—one that Sawyer had somehow rigged to make an old-fashioned *owuuuga* noise because Zack decided that was how a hippo horn would sound—echoed across the parking lot.

It was a split second before Molly realized the horn only worked if the electric golf cart was turned on. Then it happened. The cart lurched backward, bumping hard up against the curb of the sidewalk.

And bumping up just as hard against Samantha Laken, the church pianist. The blow rocked Zack from the driver's seat and sent Samantha careening to the ground.

Zack froze in utter panic. Cries of alarm went up all around the parking lot. Molly launched herself across the front of the cart to grab the little ignition key—the key she should have taken with her when she left the cart. Just as Zack began to cry and Molly clutched the key in her hand, Samantha moaned, "My arm! I think I broke my arm!"

## Chapter Eleven

"Calmed down yet?" Sawyer asked, looking as drained as Molly felt. It was nearly nine, and she'd spent the last thirty minutes trying to get Zack anywhere close to being able to sleep.

Molly collapsed into a chair at the kitchen table, where they'd tried to get Zack to eat something. "He finally nodded off about ten minutes ago." She pushed her hair out of her eyes. "He kept asking me if everyone would hate him for breaking Samantha's arm."

"He didn't break Samantha's arm," Sawyer defended. He'd been touchingly adamant in his defense of Zack's role in the accident. He'd also not left their side since it happened, even taking off from work tonight. "He didn't," he repeated.

"It's gonna be a long haul to get him to believe that." Molly couldn't decide which pressed down on her worse: the exhaustion or the disappointment. Even the second-place ribbon was lost on Zack as he wallowed in guilt and worry over what had happened.

"It isn't his fault. It was an accident." Sawyer looked

as if he'd square off against anyone who dared to say otherwise. His loyalty spoke deeply to the frayed-thin corners of her spirit.

"Why didn't I take the keys out of the cart before I let him behind the wheel? What was I thinking?" Molly's heart tore at the thought that her own carelessness had stolen Zack's glorious day right out from underneath him.

"Don't do that." Sawyer started to reach out his hand to hers, then pulled it back. She was grateful he hadn't touched her. She would have melted into him if he had—she was fighting the need to do so even now—and that would just make everything worse. "This will settle down soon enough," he said. His eyes told her he wasn't any more sure that was true than she was. But she knew how hard it was for him to be optimistic, and it touched her so that he was trying for her. "A broken arm isn't minor, but it's not a major injury, either."

"It is if you're the church piano player," Molly moaned. She certainly had no optimism left after today. "I've hurt a friend and the entire choir in one thoughtless moment. And ruined *everything* for Zack." She swiped at the tears trailing down her cheek, feeling foolish and unworthy and beyond sad.

"You didn't mean to do it. Accidents aren't the same thing as setting out to hurt someone." He paused for a moment, a faraway look in his eyes before he added, "No one remembers that."

Molly's attention snagged on the telling comment. It was the first time he'd ever come close to hinting at whatever drove him to Wander Canyon. "You know..." She kept her tone casual and gentle. "People come to

Wander Canyon because they like the idea of a friendly small town."

Sawyer sat back in his chair with a quizzical look. "What's that got to do with anything?"

Molly leaned in just a little bit. "Because from the moment I met you, I've gotten the sense you ran here to hide. From something. Or someone." She took a minute to gather her courage before asking, "Was it an accident of some kind? I mean, what you just said…"

The silence hung thick between them as Molly watched him decide how much to say. Up until today, she would have said she was skilled at keeping up a positive front. And most days, she did. But Sawyer? He was determined to hold up a barricade ten feet thick. Complete with a moat. And alligators.

"Depends on who you ask," he finally admitted. His expression was one of someone—there wasn't another word for it—captured. Cornered. The way Zack looked when he got in one of his moods and was trying to hide from her. A mix of mortification at being found and resignation that he couldn't hide forever.

"What happened?" It was hard to believe she'd never asked him before. But she'd never felt as close to Sawyer as she did right now.

Part of him wanted to tell her. She could see it, clear as day. But it would mean crossing that big moat and tearing down part of that hulking barricade. Molly found herself wishing he would find the strength to cross it. And dreading it at the same time. *It must be something terrible.* Was she ready to learn something terrible about Sawyer? Would that ruin everything?

Or simply save her from ruining everything?

There was a moment where she thought he was going to tell her. He shifted his weight, and while he kept glancing away, his gaze would always return to her.

Longing. That was what she saw in his eyes. He longed to cross the gap he'd put between himself and the world. Between himself and her. The space between them hummed with the possibility, with the wanting to and the last remnants of resistance. Molly held her breath.

And then Sawyer closed himself off again. He straightened in his chair, even drawing his arms close to his chest. "That's a conversation for some other day."

While that wasn't "I'll never tell you," it wasn't much of an invitation, either.

"We gotta fix this for Zack," he said. They both knew he was shifting back to a safer topic. "And fast."

The urgency in his words matched the worry in her own heart. "How? Samantha's already told Zack she doesn't blame him. Not that he accepts that."

Sawyer pinched the bridge of his nose, wearily grasping for some solution. She hadn't come up with anything, either. "A broken arm can't be unbroken. Samantha's going to be in that cast and unable to play piano for at least eight weeks, and we can't change that."

It hit her just then. A small burst of an idea leaped out of hiding. One she couldn't believe hadn't occurred to her sooner. They couldn't change Samantha's injury, but they could change one of the consequences. Well, *he* could. She raised an eyebrow at Sawyer.

He followed her thinking instantly, practically recoiling at the idea. "Oh no. No, not on your life."

"Why not? It would help. It would solve one piece of what's happened."

The man's frown was so fierce it was almost amusing. "I am *not* playing piano for your choir. Not in a million years."

"Come on, Sawyer. It wouldn't be forever. It'd be just until Samantha can come back."

He crossed his arms over his chest. "That could be weeks. Seriously, you can't tell me there isn't another person who can play piano in this town."

"I'm sure there is. But not one who understands Zack and was part of how we all got here in the first place." This was a good idea. Probably as much for Sawyer as for Zack. Molly wasn't going to back down. "Zack needs to see *us* putting this right," she went on. "He needs to see that when accidents happen, you don't hide in regret, you figure out how you can help fix things."

The man grunted. "That isn't a solution."

Molly fixed him with the glare sharpened by seven years of maternal convincing. "Well, no, it's not perfect. But have you got a better idea?"

# *Chapter Twelve*

An act of God.

Sawyer didn't have any other rational explanation than that for the fact he was seated behind the piano Thursday night in the sanctuary of Wander Canyon Community Church.

Well, divine intervention and Molly Kane. He tried to console himself that there wasn't a living human being who could stand up against that combination.

*You're up there laughing at me, aren't You?*

Not exactly a prayer—more like a wisecrack in the Almighty's direction—but Sawyer hoped God at least appreciated his honesty.

"Thanks for this," Pastor Newton said over Sawyer's shoulder for the tenth time. "Molly says your specialty is ragtime. I hope you'll let us hear some after practice."

Sawyer simply grunted as he turned the accompanist's hymnal to "Blessed Assurance." It had been years since his sight-reading skills had been tested—he mostly played from memory—but the simple chord structures of the hymnals posed little challenge. Anyone with basic keyboard skills could do what he was doing right now. Sawyer wasn't so sure he bought into Molly's idea that his stepping in for Samantha made a difference for Zack.

"It really is kind of you to step in," Yvonne Walker said. Sawyer remembered she was the wife Chaz was waiting on when they first met outside of the church. Which also made her Wyatt Walker's sister-in-law. Everybody really did know everybody else in this town.

"Sure you don't sing?" asked a man who introduced himself as Walt Peters. "We're desperate for baritones."

"Trust me, you're not desperate enough to need me," Sawyer replied. "My musical talents don't go any farther than these fingers."

The choir moved into "Be Thou My Vision," where Molly sang a solo. *There are some good parts to this bizarre setup,* Sawyer admitted to himself. He got to hear Molly sing up close. And he got to accompany her when she sang. It was silly to enjoy that connection as much as he did. Still, her music was so important to her, and her voice was such a gift, that a small part of him was grateful to be in the world of her music.

Her whole self lit up when Molly sang. It was like watching a high-octane version of what playing did to him—and evidently to Zack. Music soothed him, calmed him, pulled him back from the darkness that always lurked.

Molly's music didn't just soothe her, it elevated her. It took her to this joyful place he'd forgotten existed. She was beautiful in so many ways when the music filled her. Sawyer could see her faith when she sang. The word fit her: she was faith-*full* when she sang. Being able to see it so clearly in someone made it just a bit easier to believe it existed.

For other people, at least. Any faith like that still felt miles out of reach to someone like him. He'd never be faith-*full*.

But it felt good to feel *use*ful. To her as well as to Zack. Maybe Molly was right, and it would help Zack to know Sawyer had stepped up to fill Samantha's role. If nothing else, Sawyer was selfishly grateful for a reason to still be involved in their lives.

"Will you play just one?" Molly asked as they finished up rehearsal. "I want everyone to hear how good you are."

Sawyer had no doubt the pastor had put her up to it. He should head home and get a few hours' sleep in before his shift tonight, but he couldn't deny Molly anything. Especially not when she looked at him like that. The sparkle in her eyes reduced him to the kind of helplessness his dad would call smitten.

Several other choir members joined in on the pleas, so Sawyer chose a Joplin number called "Grace and Beauty" and began to play.

People were surprised, and a bit stunned. Sawyer couldn't decide if that pleased him, or if it should bother him that his abilities caught them by such surprise. It had been so long since he thought of the piano as a talent. He'd always considered it more of a survival mechanism. A way to push back against all the ugliness a man saw in law enforcement. Perhaps the way these people saw hymns and church.

"You're amazing!" Pastor Newton said. The man

looked as if he really meant it—or he was just that good at faking it.

Sawyer felt his cheeks heat at the compliment. He wasn't amazing. People like Molly were amazing, not him.

He almost wished he hadn't caught her eye after the pastor's praise. The glow in them undid him a little—a lot, maybe—as if she was proud of him. She was proud of getting him in here, probably, or of solving the problem of a rehearsal pianist. She had no reason to be proud of *him*. Still, some part of him grasped at her glee and held it tight, like a kid clutching money to buy an ice cream. Smitten, indeed.

The choir began to disperse, offering compliments and accolades as they passed by the piano bench, and Sawyer made to leave.

"Wait," Molly said.

Sawyer's whole soul—if he had one—snagged on the word, and he was caught and unable to leave even though he ought to.

"Play your favorite, would you?"

He had a dozen favorites, but he started in on the first bars of "Gladiolus Rag."

"Not ragtime." She stopped him with a hand on his shoulder. The small gesture felt enormous, and Sawyer felt himself undo a little bit more. The tightness he'd bound around himself was starting to unwind, and there didn't seem to be a single thing he could do about it. Or even wanted to. "None of those songs have words, do they?"

"No." The word choked out of him like a besotted teenager. She had no idea how beautiful she was. How would he ever be able to make this all about Zack and only Zack? "None of them."

"What's your favorite song *with* words? You must have one. Everybody does."

He knew the answer to her question in a heartbeat. But in that same heartbeat he knew it was a terrible idea to let her hear it. Like peering over a cliff to see how far the drop went down even though you were going to jump anyway.

"Don't be shy," she encouraged, probably just trying to be friendly. She had no idea what she was asking.

Sawyer put his hands to the keyboard, half praying he'd forgotten the notes.

He hadn't. Almost against his will the opening bars of Simon and Garfunkel's "Bridge Over Troubled Water" began to float out over the quiet air of the sanctuary.

Molly hummed her approval, recognizing the song. "Oh, good one." She began to hum along, and with a jolt of something very much like terror Sawyer realized she was going to start singing.

He ought to stop playing. He ought to run from the sanctuary and go home and sleep and spend the next hours in the safe dark of the security office. He ought not to accompany her sweet, clear voice singing words of grace and healing.

She began to sing, and it felt as if the whole world stopped to listen.

They were just lyrics. Words penned by famous singers decades ago. They should not have the power to cut into him like they did, to carry her voice high up into the rafters to mingle there with the chords he made.

And yet Sawyer felt utterly exposed. It was as if

the physical pain of that accident, the agony realizing what he'd done when he'd awoken in the hospital bed and the scarring of all that scorn could somehow appear all over his body, could somehow billow up like the music to fill the room.

But there, sliding wondrously through all that, was Molly's voice. Beauty singing pain. Grace singing agony. How was that even possible? How could he want to keep standing it?

When Molly's voice softened and the final chord hung delicately in the air, Sawyer felt as if he'd run a hundred miles. He stared at his fingers, stunned to find them still on the keys because he was sure they were shaking.

Somehow she knew not to speak. The raging storm in his chest must have been obvious because she knew to let the room fall to a hush. He'd always been drawn to how she could see him—*really* see him—but that felt like a blaring spotlight right now.

He tried to think of something to say. Anything normal, casual or ordinary, anything that would hide the enormity of the moment. The sheer power of emotions roiling through him. Nothing came to mind.

She leaned against the piano, waiting. For what, he wasn't sure. So even as he told himself not to, Sawyer eventually raised his gaze to hers. He expected something along the lines of "What on earth just happened?" to be in her eyes. Judgment, puzzlement or any of the hundreds of versions of morbid curiosity he'd endured in the past year.

Instead, Molly's eyes were warm. The look in them was a tender question, almost a welcome, without a hint of scorn. Care. That was what he saw in those eyes. Could it possibly be she cared for him? Sawyer absolutely, positively didn't know what to make of that.

Evidently, she did. Molly simply looked at him, nodded her head ever so slightly and said, "Welcome to church, Sawyer Bradshaw."

Without another word, she left the sanctuary, leaving Sawyer to sit there for a full thirty minutes wondering how in the world his soul had shown up now after months of being shredded and gone.

"Some kids were still mean," Zack replied when Molly asked him how the last week of school was going. They were walking back home on a gorgeous afternoon day. Things hadn't been good in the week since the festival. How could it have been? As his little backpack bobbed along over his shoulders, Molly watched the rubber band in his hands. It twisted and stretched in the nonstop fidget that had always broken her heart.

"But it's better, right?" That felt like a desperate question. Surely one or two of his classmates had to have been nice.

"Mo Winters said she liked my hippo. She said it shoulda got first prize 'cuz it was one of the biggest."

"That doesn't sound mean at all. Mo is a nice girl and a good friend." Mrs. Hollings had left a voice message on her cell phone that Zack had spent the entire lunch recess sitting alone on a bench. The image of him sitting all by himself had hounded her all afternoon.

"Billy asked me if I get to keep it."

In all the post-parade chaos of Samantha's injury, the hippo cart had, in fact, been left in the parking lot for hours until Sawyer had towed it behind his truck and parked it in her garage. "It belongs to the golf resort." Of course, it had been so radically altered she doubted the resort had much use for it now. She'd been so excited about it she'd forgotten to ask what would happen to it after the parade.

"I don't want it anyways," Zack said in sad tones. Molly was struck again how things had turned out so very differently than she'd hoped. "I'm still sad," he added with heartbreaking honesty. If his chin had sunk any lower it would be sitting on his chest.

She'd spent so much time coping with an anxious Zack, this new sad version baffled her. "I'm still sad, too," she admitted.

"Do you think Sawyer is still sad?"

"I know for a fact that he is. He was really proud of your hippo cart. Still is. What happened wasn't anyone's fault. It was…"

"I know, I know, an accident." Zack said the words as a bland recitation. "Mo said so. Everybody says so. But I wish everybody would just forget about it."

"In time they will. Nobody blames you, Zack." She was pretty sure several people blamed her—herself included—but no one blamed Zack.

It wasn't fair that the last ten seconds of a day filled with so much happiness had turned everything sour. Zack had done this brave new thing. He'd made this amazing hippo cart that had won second place. It seemed wrong that nobody remembered that.

She'd sent Steve the photo of Zack behind the wheel of the cart—a shot of the last moments before everything had gone wrong—and another later shot of the cart bearing its second place ribbon. Maybe *this one time* Steve would snap out of his heartbreaking disregard and send some sort of congratulatory note. Or call. Or anything.

Of course, nothing came.

Sawyer, on the other hand, had called after school every day this week. He'd been insistent to the point of badgering that golf lessons continue. Molly had waited for Sawyer to give her any hint as to the mountain of pain she saw well up that evening at church, but the man remained silent.

Maybe that was for the best. She was starting to feel way too much for him. They had only seen each other at The Depot in the days since the choir rehearsal, and she felt his absence keenly. He'd come to belong in many parts of her life, not just mornings at the coffee shop. She thought of him constantly. Right now, he seemed to be everything Steve wasn't—or ever would be— and that was calling to her in dangerous ways with a strength she was running out of ways to fight.

A shocking question from Zack pulled her from her thoughts. "Can I quit school? There's only four days left. It won't matter."

Molly's heart froze over. Or cracked. Or both. Zack had moaned and whined, complained and delayed, but he'd never asked to quit school before. *I pushed him too far. I got all hopeful and pushed him too far.*

She wanted to sit down on the curb and wail, but Molly told herself to keep walking and talking in calm tones. "Why do you want to quit school? You can last four days." She was pretty sure she knew why, but Molly wanted to hear how Zack would put it.

"It's no fun. Never was."

She picked up on Sawyer's favorite phrase. "Feeling lousy?"

"Yep. And not new."

No, the struggles of school were far from new to Zack. Life shouldn't be so hard at his age. Life shouldn't be so hard, period. "Lots of important things in life aren't fun. Or new."

"Why does school have to be important?" Zack whined. His little blue sneakers plodded along the sidewalk as if the walk was miles uphill in a blizzard instead of six blocks in the glorious Colorado spring sunshine. "Why can't just golf be important?"

Molly wondered what Sawyer would have to say about that statement. Was it golf that was important to Zack? Or Sawyer?

"I saw some guys on TV who were perfessonal—" Zack struggled around the large word "—golf guys. And there are grown-ups all over the golf course when everyone else is s'posed to be at work."

Molly almost had to laugh. How did this become about retirees, swanky vacationers and golf pros? "They are not in the second grade," she replied. "I expect most of them went all the way to college before their mommies and daddies let them play golf all day long." She had no idea if that was true of golf pros, but it was at least plausible so it served her point. "Even Sawyer doesn't play golf all day long. He has important work to do."

Zack shifted his backpack and began working the rubber band again. "He works all by himself," he said with admiration. Then he muttered, "He doesn't have Davey Jacobs saying he drives a killer hippo."

Molly stopped walking. "A killer hippo? Is that what Davey Jacobs said to you?" What kind of an unfair crack was that? Molly's heart burned. Davey Jacobs had been Zack's nemesis since kindergarten. A handsome, outspoken and astoundingly mean little boy who bullied Zack and any other kid he could find. A mini version of his boisterous, boasting father, actually. While Molly ought to know better, the Jacobses were one of the few school families she had never invited to church. It was cowardly to protect church as the one place where Zack didn't have to worry about Davey Jacobs, and she was ashamed of her shortcoming. All the ways church could help Sawyer stood out crystal clear to her, but Molly could never muster the compassion to see the ways church could probably help Davey Jacobs.

"Part of growing up is learning how to deal with other people. Even the ones we don't like or are mean to us."

Zack shot her a "moms are supposed to say stuff like that" look. He had a point—Sawyer hadn't seemed to learn the lesson about dealing with other people. The man walked around as if the whole world was his own personal unfriendly second grade. Maybe that was how he had connected with Zack so quickly and with such intensity.

"Can't I just grow up and work all by myself like Sawyer?"

Molly pondered how to answer that until an idea came to her. "Think about Pastor Newton. He has to work with all kinds of people, sometimes when they are very mad or very sad. Does he seem happy to you?"

"Well, yeah. But he's s'posed to be."

Molly could go into all the ways she felt happiness was a choice more than a personality trait, but that wasn't the argument to have with someone with Zack's anxieties. She knew Zack would choose to be less anxious if it really was a choice. She always had to remind herself that, for reasons she didn't understand, God had wired Zack with a collection of fears other people didn't have.

"And Sawyer," she went on. "He's all by himself, just like you say. Does he seem happy to you?" It would do no good to have Zack idolize Sawyer's self-imposed exile.

"Not happy like *you*," Zack said. He sounded way too much like a teenager mortified by his mom. She knew those years were coming, but they didn't have to show up now.

"Sawyer is a sad man in lots of ways that don't have anything to do with how many people are around him. Just like Pastor Newton is a happy man, which doesn't have anything to do with how much time he spends with people from church." She felt compelled to drive the point home. "So quitting school to play golf all by yourself won't solve your problems." Inspired, she added, "Most people play golf in sets of four, you know. It's not a by-yourself kind of game."

Sawyer clearly hadn't told him this. Zack looked betrayed. Of course, Mrs. Hollings had envisioned it as a solo sport right now for Zack's purposes, so why would

Sawyer bring up golf leagues or the fact that many high schools and colleges had golf teams?

"I just wanna play the way Sawyer and I play."

"And you can," Molly replied. "Just not as a replacement for second grade. After-school lessons are fine, but they'll stay *after* school."

"I like 'em," Zack said. His steps picked up again, and Molly breathed a sigh of relief that maybe this dark moment had passed. For now. "They're not lousy anymore. Or new." He looked up at her. "I won't have to stop ever, will I?"

And there it was: that question Molly had feared from the beginning. Sawyer had never struck her as the kind of man to stick around. Once whatever he was running from caught up with him—and it would, because things like that always do—he'd be gone.

She left the question unanswered. The last thing Zack needed was another man disappearing from his life with barely a trace.

For that matter, it was the last thing she needed, as well.

# Chapter Thirteen

"Killer hippo?!" Sawyer wanted to go find that Jacobs kid and give him a piece of his mind.

Molly took her hands off the cart. They were getting ready to push it out of her garage Wednesday onto the flatbed truck for him to take it back to the resort. "I knew it was a mistake to tell you. It's almost funny. Now." She stepped back and eyed the hippo face. "If we just paint a set of angry eyebrows over here…"

"All kinds of wrong," Sawyer shot back in defense of the hippo's goofy happy face. No way was he having any part of dismissing this kid's mean remark. "Where was the teacher during all this?"

Molly's sigh spoke volumes. "Kids like Davey Jacobs are always really good at slipping cracks like that in when the teacher can't see or hear them. And it just gets worse if Zack tells on him. But I won't say I don't have a dozen unsent mean letters to Doris Jacobs sitting in my bureau drawer."

Sawyer could just imagine. "You don't send them?"

She sat back against a beat-up filing cabinet that

stood against one wall. "Doris isn't the problem. Well, the fact that Doris won't stand up to her husband—who's just a Davey in grown-up clothes if you ask me—that's the problem."

Sawyer had met guys like Davey's dad back on the force. Multiple times a week. Quick to build themselves up, and always at someone else's expense. It burned him that this crack had been at Zack's expense, and that Molly had been hurt by it, as well. "The guy sounds like a real prince."

Molly looked him right in the eye. "Not all men are." She held his gaze for a long time—way longer than his gut could stand. Her eyes said things that called to him, things that didn't match with all the "keep your distance" commands she'd given him earlier.

Sawyer leaned back against the opposite wall and shifted to another subject. A question that had been bugging him for a while now. "Does Zack miss his dad?"

The woman wore her heart on her sleeve. Pain and disappointment pulled her features down, draining all the fire out of her eyes. It made Sawyer want to give Steve Kane a bigger piece of his mind than the one aimed at Jacobs.

"Of course he does." There was so much resignation in her voice. And from a woman who seemed unlikely to resign to anything.

"Does he tell you that?"

"He tries not to. He asks me questions he thinks will hide it." She sighed and wrung her hands, a gesture just a bit of an echo of Zack's fidgeting. "But it's so obvious he wants Steve's attention that I yell into my pillow some nights."

He couldn't picture sweet Molly Kane yelling at anybody, even though it sounded like this Steve deserved it. Sawyer's gut twisted at the idea that some jerk like Davey's dad paid all kinds of attention while Steve couldn't muster up a shred of attention for a kid like Zack.

It didn't take a shrink to connect the dots. At least some of Zack's anxieties had to stem from having no dad to count on. And perhaps—even though the thought made him gulp—why Zack had glommed on to him so hard and fast. And Molly? He looked at her and saw a loneliness alike and yet totally different from his own. That made him gulp, too.

"Hard on your own?" he asked, finding the words awkward and way too simple for a huge issue like that. Some people, like him, were wired for isolation. Molly was wired for people, and lots of them.

She paused before answering, and the silence told him just how hard it was. He watched her try to find some sunny way to put it, some optimistic Molly-esque answer with a silver lining.

She couldn't. Her swallow was as hard as his, and Sawyer realized what a painful question he'd asked.

"I'm sorry." Again, the words were so insufficient to what he wanted to say.

She sniffed and pulled in a breath big enough to make Sawyer wonder how close she'd been to crying.

"I think you're doing an amazing job with him. Really." He watched how the compliment struck her, soft and startled, as if she didn't get many of them. How could people not be piling on the praise to someone like her, handling Zack's complexities the way she did?

What kind of idiot discarded a woman like her and a boy like Zack? *Steve's a fool*, he wanted to shout. *You're wonderful. You deserve so much better.*

In that moment, staring at how she blinked back tears, a foolhardy part of him desperately wanted to be that so much better. Which was, of course, desperately utter nonsense. Even if Molly hadn't drawn that big fat line in the sand between them, Sawyer was smart enough to know she was way out of his league. Zack deserved a dad with his act together, and that wasn't him. Molly deserved someone good and kind and noble and filled with faith, and that wasn't him. He'd just have to content himself with being allowed to linger in the glow of her light for a little while. Only linger, because he wasn't dumb enough to think he could stay.

Molly looked at him with such compassion that for a second Sawyer worried he'd spoken his thoughts aloud.

"You've been doing a pretty amazing job with him, too, you know. He'd never have even tried to build the hippo if you hadn't helped."

"And look what happened."

"What happened?" she asked.

"You were there, you know what happened."

"No, I mean to you. What happened?"

Sawyer had been dreading the moment she asked. And she chose to ask him *now*? He couldn't bring himself to answer.

Molly hugged her chest. "It's something awful, isn't it?"

*Tell her*, some dark voice said. *Tell her and it will all be over.* Only he couldn't bear for it to be over. Not just yet. Now it was his turn to hesitate on an answer. From somewhere way down below all that yearning he found the hard wall he put around himself and yanked it back up between them. "I'd better get this back to the resort."

He began to push the golf cart toward the truck, forcing himself not to look at her. He'd gotten the thing another two feet before he felt her hand on his shoulder. The tender touch seared like a burn.

"What happened, Sawyer?"

It was the way she said his name that did him in. Filled with kindness, as if he was redeemable. Nothing was less true in all the world.

"Something terrible." Sawyer made himself promise not to say any more than that.

"I don't think terrible things make terrible people."

He didn't reply. What reply was there to an upstanding thought like that? Even before the accident, he'd never been that glass-half-full kind of optimist. He certainly wasn't now. Knowing she was expecting an answer, he gave her a murky grunt that let her know she wasn't going to get one.

"That's the whole point of mercy," she said. "We never deserve it. And the whole point of God is that He gives it anyway."

*Now who's the idiot?* he chided himself silently. *Look at you. So ready to think she's thinking about you as a man, and she's just thinking about you as someone who ought to be in church.*

"I'm not somebody you can fix," he said more bitterly than she deserved. He turned and pushed the cart up the ramps onto the flatbed.

"Sawyer..."

*Stop saying my name like that,* he pleaded silently as he tied down the cart as fast as he could.

"Zack and I won't give up on you." The defiance in her words snuck in under the thick wall and made him want to believe things he had no business believing.

*You should, Molly. You should.*

Tessa looked concerned as she sat in Molly's kitchen the next day. "Are you sure you want me to do this?"

Molly looked out the window where Greg and Zack were celebrating the end of the school year by goofing around with the three golf holes in her backyard. "Yes. I have to know what happened to Sawyer. And he's not saying."

"I'm not a private investigator. If you didn't find anything doing an internet search, I may not come up with anything, either."

Molly sighed and put Zack's backpack away in the top of the closet. She'd had Tessa and Greg come over on the pretense of the end-of-school celebration, but it really was just to ask for Tessa's help. "You're a reporter, so that's the next best thing, right?"

Tessa smirked. "I'm a reporter for a dinky little community newspaper. Don't overestimate my skills here."

"What I won't overestimate is your heart. If there's something to find, you'll find it."

Tessa stacked folders and notebooks and put them into a box on the kitchen table. "Maybe it's *your* heart I ought to be worried about. He's getting to you, isn't he?"

"No," Molly answered quickly.

"Come on. Everything he's done for Zack? The golf

holes and that amazing cart?" Tessa leaned in. "*And a musician!* I always knew you'd fall for a musician."

"I am not falling for him. I'm grateful to him."

Tessa laughed. "And I'm the Queen of England. Don't ever play cards, Molly. Your eyes give you away every time. Mysterious and handsome can be quite a combination."

Molly walked away, suddenly needing something in a kitchen drawer.

"Look, he's been helpful and you've been holding everything up on your own for a long time. Nobody would fault you for liking someone who's great with Zack. You're being smart and checking the guy out. We both know he's hiding something, so best to know what that is."

Molly turned back to Tessa. "What if it's awful? Really 'don't ever go near my son ever again' awful?"

"Are you asking me if I think Sawyer is a serial killer?"

"No. Well, maybe." It felt absurd to admit that.

"The thing about digging up someone's past," Tessa said, "is that you have to be ready for what you find. You asked him if it was terrible and he said yes. Maybe he just thinks it's terrible, but maybe it really is."

"Which is why I have to know," Molly insisted.

Tessa planted her hands on her hips. "So ask him."

"I did."

"Ask him like you really mean it. Come on, Molly, I've seen you be relentless about things way less important. Don't you think whatever it is would be way better coming from him?"

"He's not going to tell me." After a pause she admitted, "And I have to know."

That brought a raised eyebrow from Tessa. "Because…"

Was she ready to admit it? Especially to Tessa? That was probably a moot question, because the look on Tessa's face showed she had already guessed. "I need reasons not to like him."

"Are we talking Molly 'friendly person' like? Or Molly 'lonely woman who deserves someone who truly cares' like?"

"That isn't a real question. I don't even know what that means." Molly tried to make it sound like a snappy comeback, but it fell short.

Tessa leaned her elbows on the counter. "Oh, I think you do. Totally. So are these feelings that we're pretending don't exist mutual?"

"I don't know."

"I don't buy that for a second. You have more intuition about people than anyone else I know. Which means it *is* mutual, and that scares you."

Maybe talking about it would tamp down the low hum of connection she felt to Sawyer. The low hum that wasn't staying low at all. These days it felt as if it were roaring in her ears. "He's so good with Zack. He gets him in ways I can't. How is that possible? I'm his mother."

"Don't make this about Zack. How is he with you? I heard you the other day, you know. I had to pick up some papers from the church office after choir rehearsal and I passed by the sanctuary on my way out. I heard you singing. That wasn't about church. And it wasn't about Zack."

Molly felt her cheeks flush. "You heard that?"

Tessa's voice grew tender. "I did. And it was stunning. Beauty like that doesn't come out of nowhere."

Molly sat down on one of the counter stools. "He looks at me like I'm…important. He treats the simple act of my getting his coffee every morning like some kind of enormous gift. I like to think I'm nice to everybody, but Sawyer treats me like I'm the only person who is ever nice to him. As if it means everything to him. As if *I* mean everything to him." She grimaced at Tessa. "I can't mean that much to him, can I?"

Tessa joined her at the other stool. "Maybe you are the only person who's kind to him. He works at Mountain Vista and I've never seen him talk to anyone else. Well, he does a little bit now, and somehow I think you had a lot to do with that. And the piano thing? No one knew he was so talented until you figured it out and put it to use. You're changing him. You do that to people, if you hadn't noticed."

"I touched him." It blurted out of her, awkward and sudden. "Last night as we were putting the golf cart on the truck while Zack was at the church kids group. There was so much pain and loneliness in his face and he'd told me I was an amazing mother and I put my hand on his shoulder."

Tessa's eyes widened. "And?"

"Zing. High-voltage, 'all the way down to your toes' zing. Him, too. Scared the living daylights out of both of us." She felt an echo of the sensation just remembering the moment. "That's why I have to know."

"It's no crime to be attracted to a handsome man who pays attention to you," Tessa replied. "And if it's that strong, you're smart to want to know what's behind all that mysterious, brooding pain." She gave the last words a dramatic emphasis. "I'll admit, he doesn't seem your type, but then again I thought Steve was perfect for you and look what happened there."

Molly looked out at her son playing with Greg. They were now devising some sort of golf ball race, knocking them around the three holes like barrel racers at the rodeo. "I can't let Zack get hurt again. I can't get hurt again. I need to be way more careful than I feel." She put a hand on Tessa's shoulder, unnerved by the reminder of how she'd done that to Sawyer and the feelings it created. "You'll help?"

Tessa pulled her into a hug. "Of course I will. I'll find out everything I can." She pulled back and gave Molly a look. "But is it okay if I say a prayer that whatever it is isn't enough to blow up what's cooking between you two?"

That was Tessa, always seeing through right to the heart of things. "Go ahead. I've actually been praying the same thing."

## *Chapter Fourteen*

Molly told herself to treat Sawyer like every other customer Friday morning. She hadn't seen him since their last meeting, and Zack had his first post-school lesson with him this afternoon. While part of her knew you couldn't exactly press Rewind on something like this, she was going to try.

"Good morning," she called too cheerily to Sawyer as he pushed through the door.

He looked awful. Weary and tense. "Can we put an extra shot in there this morning?"

Three shots of espresso was a lot, even for a guy his size. "Sure," she said. She might have added, "What's wrong?" for any other customer, but she didn't for him. "Extra jolt, coming right up."

"Thanks."

The awkwardness between them bothered her, but Molly tried to reason that it was safer than the simmering connection she'd felt the other night. *The distance between you is your ally right now*, she told herself. *You don't know enough, and he's not telling.*

"Zack will see you at two thirty?" she asked. It seemed too cautious, even cruel, that she'd not said, "We'll see you."

He noticed. Why wouldn't he? He always paid careful attention to everything about her. Guilt at her cowardice poked under her ribs as she added the third shot and handed over the coffee.

He fished in his pocket for the extra charge for a third shot, but she waved him off. "Still on the house." Molly told herself she would have done that for any customer looking like he'd had the day—or the night—Sawyer had.

He nodded in thanks, then started to leave. Halfway to the door he stopped and then turned back. "Did Steve ever get back to you or Zack at all about the parade? The ribbon?"

It wasn't fair how the question sliced at her. Why had she even told Sawyer she'd sent it to Steve? She should have known her ex wouldn't reply. She should have known she was setting herself up for disappointment, done in by her own insistent optimism.

"No." She didn't quite hide the anger in her answer, nor did Sawyer hide his disgust at Steve's inattention. Her heart snagged on how he seemed ready to stand in her defense. Her heart was going a lot of places it shouldn't these days.

"Does Zack know? I mean, in case he brings it up." It was as if Sawyer was apologizing for caring. Here this guy was making excuses for caring too much while Steve couldn't be bothered to care at all. Some days it stunned her how she'd ever loved Steve.

"No," she replied. The weight of the word didn't need any further explanation.

Sawyer took a step back toward her. "Do you think you could maybe send me a photo of the ribbon with Zack this afternoon? The resort wanted to put the golf cart on display, and I think the ribbon should be with it. If it's okay with you, that is."

Another gesture that pulled at her resistance. How lovely would it be for Zack to see his cart on display with the ribbon at the resort when he went for lessons? Everyone was so quick to cast Mountain Vista as this merciless corporate giant. Maybe they weren't as bad as all that. "Of course." Had Mountain Vista offered? Or had Sawyer asked? Maybe it was better if she didn't know.

Sawyer nodded. "Okay, then. I'll see Zack this afternoon. We'll try to make it a good day." They were struggling to have something close to a regular conversation, but it wasn't working. There was so much unsaid, so much hiding behind the pauses and deflected looks. And to try to pretend that the simmering connection wasn't there? Well, that was just about useless.

Molly watched him walk out the door, down the little steps from the train-car coffee shop. For a moment he sipped his coffee and stared at the big red barnlike structure that held the carousel. Did he regret it? Getting involved, saying yes to helping Zack? Saying yes to the golf lessons? Molly knew she'd dragged him into something way more complicated than the simple "Can you teach my son to hit a golf ball" request she'd made five weeks ago. But how could she have known the connection he'd have with Zack? The powerful effect he had on her son?

The powerful effect he was having on her?

Molly shook off the admission and began wiping down the espresso machine with vigor. *Don't go there. You don't know what he's hiding. That man is a mountain of pain and guilt, and that's the last thing you need. Keep it to golf teacher. Well, and choir pianist. And coffee shop regular.*

And right there was the problem: the list of things Sawyer Bradshaw was to her kept growing.

*Lord*, she prayed as the next customer came in the door, *You know what he's hiding. Show me what I need to know.*

Sawyer stared at his cell phone late that afternoon, a few hours after Zack had left. Sitting on the screen of the phone was the number for Detective Dana Preston. His finger had hovered over the icon to connect half a dozen times, but he'd been unable to bring himself to press Call.

He'd not called anyone from his old Denver Police Department in months, even though Dana had left several messages. They'd been something close to friends, and she'd been one of the few people who didn't disappear into thin air after everything had gotten messed up.

Then again, *he'd* done the disappearing.

It felt like a monumental thing to call Dana, but every moment Sawyer had spent in Zack's company this afternoon had screamed "Do something!" to him. The boy was so beaten down. Reverting back to something too close to the jittery, closed-off little guy he'd first met.

Life had piled up an unfair heap of obstacles in front of Zack, and it bugged Sawyer endlessly not to be able to pull some of them down.

And he had pulled some of them down, hadn't he? He liked to think golf was working. Zack was getting okay at it, and you could say they were having fun. He was proud of that.

Sawyer also found himself dangerously proud of Zack's work on the hippo cart. He was equally ticked off at how it had all turned out. It scared him how invested he'd become in Zack. How angry he was on the boy's behalf.

But it didn't end there. Something was lurking under all that—lurking under everything, probably—that wouldn't leave Sawyer alone. The kid just wanted someone to care about him. Someone other than his mom, because, well, moms were supposed to care. They *had* to, right?

Shouldn't dads have to, as well?

Even he could see what Zack was doing in their time together. For whatever misguided reason, Zack had latched on to him as a stand-in for all the attention his father was denying him. Maybe it was their similar personalities, the isolation or some ill-advised twist of fate. Molly would surely put it down to God and answered prayer.

He was not the answer to Molly's prayers for Zack. That person should be Steve. Someone had to wake Steve up to his inexcusable absence and make him pay attention.

*I can't be what Zack wants*, Sawyer told himself. *But*

*maybe I can get him what he needs.* He hit the button to connect the call.

"Sawyer?" Dana's usually low voice pitched up in surprise. "Whoa, Sawyer, is this really you?"

"Yeah," he said, suddenly feeling stupid. Why had he thought this was a good idea?

Her voice softened again. "Where are you? Are you okay? You dropped off the planet after..." She didn't finish the sentence.

Sawyer paced a bit, working up his nerve. "I know. I needed to get out of there. I'm fine." He didn't really know if he was fine, but this call wasn't about him.

"Nobody's fine after what happened to you." Not too many people understood the weight of what had happened to him, but Dana always had. She had incredible instincts about people. It was what made her such a great detective. Her work with abused kids would have made most people hard and bitter, but she'd managed to stay open and human. Sawyer hoped that would work in his favor.

"I'm okay, really. But listen, I need a favor."

That sent her radar off. "So you're not okay."

"No, really," he insisted. "I'm all right. Promise. But I need to find someone and I'm hoping you can help."

"You're not in any kind of trouble?"

For a woman with no kids of her own, Dana mothered everybody. "No, *Mom*, I'm fine," he teased her by calling her Mom the way he always had. It felt good to do some tiny thing from his old life. "I need to find a kid's dad. Can you do that?"

"Is there a mom in the picture?"

"Yes. She's..." he balked for a minute, stumped for

how to classify Molly "…someone I know. The dad's checked out, and the boy is hurting on account of it. She's given up on her ex, but I…" His words fell off. Suddenly his plan felt like a giant dose of ill-advised meddling.

"You want to help reunite this little guy with his dad?"

It would have been better if Dana didn't sound so shocked. Good deeds weren't that far out of his wheelhouse, were they? "Well, yeah."

The pause on Dana's end of the phone made his skin itch. "This isn't some kind of penance, is it? You've got nothing to make up for, Sawyer."

He didn't see it that way, but now wasn't the time to get into that. Besides, lots of people didn't see it that way, so no point in trying to convince Dana.

"I'm just trying to help a kid out, okay? His mom works at the shop where I get my coffee." That sounded innocent enough. "He's seven, his dad doesn't give him the time of day and it would feel good to set it right."

Dana sighed. "You probably can't. You know that, don't you?"

"I want to try. Come on, haven't you ever just wanted to give something a last-ditch try?" He knew that would get her. Dana was a sucker for a lost cause, especially when it came to kids.

He could practically hear the detective narrow her eyes at him over the phone. "All right, then. Have you got a name?"

"Steve Kane. With a *K*. Mid-to-late thirties, formerly married to Molly Kane. Kid's name is Zack." An odd chill of nervous exposure raced down his back at giving away that information.

"Have you got an address?" she asked.

Sawyer stopped pacing. "Well, if I had this guy's address and phone number I wouldn't be calling you, now, would I?"

"For *them*," Dana insisted. Sawyer cringed and hoped she couldn't sense how far out of his comfort zone this ask was for him.

He gave Molly's address, his mind pulling up the sight of the cluttered garage and the wacky little golf course in the backyard. The places where he'd always lived were *housing*. Every little touch about Molly's house made it a *home*. He wanted to spend more time in that home so badly it scared him.

"Sawyer." Dana's mom voice was back. "I hate to ask, but mind telling me what you're going to do when you find this guy?"

He wasn't ready to explain that. He wasn't even sure he knew the answer anyway. "The little guy needs his dad." The words came out too thick, as if the raw emotion of them caught in his throat. "Somebody needs to convince Steve Kane to pay attention to his son."

"And why is that someone you?"

This was why he'd hesitated calling Dana. She'd analyze the living daylights out of why he was doing this, and there weren't reasons. Not ones he wanted analyzed anyway.

Sawyer started pacing again, trying to find some way to explain his urgency without having to explain his feelings. "I like Zack. I've been teaching him to play golf and…"

"You *what*?" Dana cut him off midsentence.

Sawyer squinted his eyes shut. "His mom asked me

because I work at the golf resort out here. He didn't need real lessons, just someone to show him the basics. He's a good kid—really smart—just really…nervous. Worries about everything, you know?"

"Including why his dad isn't in his life?"

"I don't know that he worries about that, as much as he's just disappointed." Frustration twisted Sawyer's gut. "I just want to help him, and this is the way I think I can. Molly won't hunt this jerk down and tell him to step up to the plate."

"So you will." Dana's statement sounded more like she clearly thought it wasn't a good idea.

"So I'm *willing* to," he countered. "This kid needs his dad."

"Every child has a father," Dana replied. "Some of them definitely *don't* need the dads biology gave them." He knew she spoke from experience. Dana had seen the worst of what a parent's attention—or neglect—could do. "If you care enough about this Zack to go hunt down his dad, maybe you care enough about him to fill the hole his dad has left."

"No." He hoped Dana would leave it at that.

She didn't. "Maybe it's time to crawl out of that valley you dug for yourself. Helping this kid could be a first step. How much longer are you going to stay wherever it is you are playing unworthy hermit?"

There were days he hated Dana's ability to turn a phrase. "I'm not here to make friends."

"Sounds like you've made two. Why is that so awful?"

Sawyer swallowed his urge to toss the phone across the room. "Are you going to help me or not?"

"Relax," Dana replied. "I'll help. I just want you to

think about the fact that you may already have what the kid needs while you're going on some wild-goose chase for help that isn't coming. Fathers like that don't change."

"I just need to know I've done what I can."

"That's just it, Bradshaw. You haven't. You *can* do something—something really important—but you won't admit it."

"Call me when you have the info?" It was long past time for this conversation to be over.

"I will." After a pause, Dana added, "It was good to hear from you. I miss arguing with your grumpy mug."

They'd been good friends. Everyone always thought it was going to turn into something more, but there'd never been any hint of that sort of thing between them. She was like his little sister. His bossy, know-it-all little sister.

He was taking a breath to say goodbye when she asked, "Will you come back? Ever?"

Sawyer pushed out a long breath. All the missing hours of sleep felt like they caught up with him in one instant. "I don't know."

"You can, you know." Her voice was too gentle. "You can always come back."

Sawyer rushed through a quick goodbye and ended the call. He sat for a long time in the corner of his sad, sterile little kitchen. The shadows grew long across the wall as one thought hung thin and hollow in the air.

*I don't think that's true.*

# *Chapter Fifteen*

Molly wiped the shower mist away from the bathroom mirror, stared at her pale face and tried to remember how to breathe.

*No. Dear God in Heaven, no.*

Her fear was too shocked for tears, too bone-deep even for words. She moved her hand over again to the spot a few inches under her left collarbone, pleading for her fingers to lie to her.

Small, round, unnatural. The lump shouted *Catastrophe!* at her from just under her skin.

She couldn't stop the instant response, no matter how irrational it was: *I'm going to die.* Followed immediately by the overwhelming horror of *I'm going to leave Zack all alone.* Some small distant part of her knew that was far from certain, that she was overreacting on insufficient information, but none of that could get through the thick fog of fear.

Molly's head spun while her vision sharpened. She gripped the sink, worried she might faint. The outside world was just as it had been moments before, the happy launch-of-summer ease of Memorial Day still lingering in the air. And now everything was completely different. She thought of the moments just before an avalanche, where the snow lay perfectly still before a crack ran across its surface. And then everything slid downhill. Crashed downhill, burying anything and anyone in its path.

She sank down onto the rim of the tub, thoughts scurrying in a dozen panicked directions. She wanted to cry out, to sob or howl or something, but shock closed her throat. A blessing, perhaps, as Zack was twenty feet away at the breakfast counter, happily munching French toast as if it were an ordinary morning.

No ordinary morning. A dreaded, desperately feared morning. Molly gulped for air, reaching for a foothold that wouldn't come.

*You don't know*, she tried to tell herself. *You don't know. It could be anything. It could be nothing. You don't know.* The thunder of her pulse in her ears refused to listen.

Molly forced herself to stand, staring hard at the terrified woman in the mirror. She tried to command that feeble woman to get a grip on herself. She leaned over and splashed cold water on her face twice, three times.

"Mom!" Zack's voice cut through both the closed bathroom door and the fog around her. "What if I don't like day camp?"

How little and impossible that fear seemed in the light of what threatened to pull her under just now.

"You'll be fine," she called, then almost sobbed for the lie that suddenly felt like. *It won't be fine. How can it be fine?* "Go get dressed."

Turning back to her reflection, Molly gave whispered orders. "Get him to day camp. Call Dr. Swanson after you get him to the community center. Just get that far. That's all you have to do. You can do that. God, help me do that."

Molly moved through the motions of getting Zack off to summer day camp in a stunned blur. She packed a lunch and checked his backpack on autopilot, barely able to think about it. She was grateful for the spring rain, as it meant they could drive rather than walk. She didn't have it in her to go through the long list of concerns Zack posed today.

He noticed. "Mom?" he asked as they turned into the community center parking lot. Zack looked at her with worried eyes.

"Yes, hon?" She hoped she sounded cheery.

"You okay? You seem...I dunno...weird."

She tried to give him a playful smile. "I'm always weird, right?"

He wasn't buying it. "I have a bit of a headache this morning," she offered. "Must be the rainstorm. A little coffee should clear that right up, won't it?" The sharp edge of her lie cut into her heart.

She instantly realized she should never have said anything even remotely medical. Zack's eyes went wide. "Are you sick?"

Molly had been careful to never refer to anything of that sort in front of Zack. Granted, he only had a seven-year-old's understanding of cancer and remission and reoccurrence, but he could spin that into a storm of worries in a heartbeat. She was watching it right in front of her eyes.

"No, sweetheart." Another lie. Or possible lie. A kind one, if nothing else. "Grown-ups get headaches all the time. It's why we sell so much coffee at The Depot."

"So you're not sick?"

She gave his hair a playful ruffle. "What I am is worried you'll be late for your first day of summer camp. Get on in there and have a wonderful day, okay? Come home and tell me all about it."

"Sure." His reply sounded anything but sure.

Molly waved Zack off, pulled her car off the road two blocks away, and sobbed.

It was 9:20 a.m. on a Tuesday and Molly wasn't here. She was supposed to be here, and she wasn't. "Double-shot Americano," he told the young man behind the counter.

"Oh, yeah. You." As the man began making the drink, Sawyer debated how odd it would look to ask where Molly was. "Molly called in sick at the last minute," he offered, solving Sawyer's problem.

"Zack again? I thought school was out," he said.

"Didn't say."

Something was wrong. He could feel it in his gut, as if he'd suddenly gained Molly's famous intuition. But what could he do about it? He hadn't earned the right to get involved in her life.

The idiocy of that statement hit him as he waited for his coffee. Get involved? Hadn't his phone call to Dana been a heap of involved?

Whatever she was going through, she was doing too much of it alone. Zack was doing too much of it alone. The lack of support in her life was making him absurdly worried. The urge to protect her, to care for her, was chasing him, no matter how he tried to outrun it.

*That can't be you*, he lectured himself as the espresso machine hissed. *She has friends. Lots of them, from the looks of it. What could you possibly add to that?*

It did little good. As he got back into his truck, Sawyer dialed Molly's phone number even as he told himself not to. He grunted as it went to voice mail, and ended the call. He couldn't bring himself to leave a "Where are you? Call me?" message on account of how meddling that would sound.

He slipped his good-but-not-quite-Molly-perfect coffee in the cupholder and started to drive home. Instead, he somehow ended up steering his truck through the streets of Wander Canyon, searching for Molly's little blue car. It was probably best that he didn't find it, because he had no idea of what he'd do if he came across her. The power of his inappropriate worry for her drove him into a panic worthy of Zack's anxious fits.

*You'd keep her safe, wouldn't You?* It was more of a demand than a prayer. As if he had any business making demands of a God he'd ignored for years. Still, God seemed so precious to Molly that Sawyer had to believe Molly was precious to God.

Just as he was heading for home, Sawyer's cell phone rang. He practically slammed his hand on the button that connected the call in his truck, sure it was Molly.

It wasn't. It had no reason to be. But it was Dana Preston.

"I got your guy," she said. "Check your email. It's not much, but address and cell phone should be enough for what you want." Her voice held a strong tint of *Don't make me regret doing this*.

That timing had to be God-sent, right? Handing him a way to talk to Steve just when Molly might need him most? If he moved the needle even a little bit on Steve's attention, it would do a world of good for both mother and son. He could be useful here in a way that would make a permanent difference in their lives.

"Thanks, Dana," he replied. "Much appreciated."

"Sawyer?" Dana's mother voice was back.

"Yeah?"

"Don't do something stupid when the wiser choice is staring you in the face."

"Another lecture," he muttered.

"One you need," she countered. "Are you gonna let me know what happens?"

"Probably not."

Now it was she who muttered, "I don't know why I keep holding out hope for you."

"Now who's making the stupid choice when the wiser one is staring you in the face?" It had always been fun to throw Dana's words back at her. Sawyer discovered it had lost its appeal in this case. "I gotta go. I got a phone call to make."

He did. He wasn't sure how, or if it even stood a chance of working, but so help him he would give it everything he had to try.

# Chapter Sixteen

Molly stormed up the stairs to the little apartment above the barbershop Wednesday and pounded on the door. Loud. He might be asleep at this time of day but she didn't care. "Sawyer!"

After another minute of calling he came to the door. His groggy expression changed the moment he caught sight of hers. "How did you do that? How *could* you do that?" she started in immediately. She wasn't in the mood for small talk. Not with him. "How could you possibly think it was okay to do that?"

At least he showed her the decency of not asking "Do what?" He knew exactly what she was asking about.

"You want to come in?" he asked, looking down the long stairway as if someone else might be watching below. Wander was always watching, but no one was here now.

"No, I don't want to come in, I want to know why on earth you felt you could contact Steve? Do you have any idea what you've done?"

"Why haven't you ever demanded he pay more attention to Zack? How do you let him get away with disappointing Zack like that?"

Shock at Sawyer's bold question flashed through her chest. "What business is it of yours?"

"You see it, don't you? Come on, if even I can see it, surely you see it. It's killing him that Steve ignores him."

Molly stormed into the apartment, ready to have it out. She hadn't been this angry in ages, and she was far too stressed to cut Sawyer any slack for good intentions. "So you think the answer is for you—*you*—to just haul off and demand attention from Steve?"

"Someone needs to set him straight. I thought I'd try."

Molly was momentarily struck by the dark, bleak room Sawyer called home. It was so impersonal, so sparse. More empty than a hotel room or even a dormitory. It was a split-second impression, a flash interruption of her anger. "Without asking me. Inappropriate doesn't even begin to cover it. I'm not even sure it isn't illegal."

Sawyer shut the door behind them. "I didn't break any laws. I had a detective friend find him. I gave him a call and he picked up. I didn't go down to Denver and stalk him, if that's what you're thinking."

"You can't do that!" Molly couldn't believe she had to explain this to him.

"Well, no, it's not a perfect solution, but…"

"It's not a solution *at all*. I don't know what you thought you'd accomplish, but all you've done is tick Steve off. If there was ever any hope at all that he'd come around, you've just killed it." She forced herself to look directly at him. "You know, I thought you cared about Zack." She was furious, yes, but she was also disappointed. It felt as if everything was going to pieces.

"Why have you never demanded he get involved?" Sawyer asked again. "Why have you just lain down and accepted how he's acting? You don't do that with anyone else."

She pointed at him. "You've got a lot of nerve, mister." His question infuriated her. "I will not *beg* for Zack's father's affections. I will not force Steve to play at fatherhood only to watch him disappoint Zack time after time."

Sawyer pointed right back. "He's *already* disappointing Zack. It needs to stop. And if I have to tick the guy off by telling him what he should already know, then I'm okay with that. He can hate me instead of you and Zack. I'd do that for him. I've got a particular talent for being hated."

She had promised herself she wasn't going to bring this up now, but he'd opened the door. "So I've heard."

That stopped Sawyer cold. His whole body stiffened for a moment, then his shoulders sagged. He'd known this was coming, she realized. He'd been waiting for it.

"You know." The words were a surrender. The defeat she heard in them still managed to tug at her despite all the anger boiling inside.

"I know what you wouldn't tell me, yes." After a second she dared to add, "It would have been so much better coming from you." Actually, she couldn't say if that was true. She just knew it hurt that he didn't trust her enough to tell her. It also made it easier to believe she'd been right in keeping an emotional distance between them. Or at least trying to. She was wounded enough now to recognize she hadn't succeeded in that at all. It stung badly because she cared deeply. What a whopping mess this whole thing had become.

Sawyer turned to face the window, slumping wearily. "Who told you?" He tossed the words out as if it really didn't matter how she knew. As if he'd been trying to hold back an avalanche by not telling her. And wasn't that exactly what he'd been trying to do? Everyone in Wander Canyon—everyone in Colorado, for that matter—knew you couldn't hold back an avalanche. You could only keep out of its path. Careful as she'd been, she hadn't managed to stay out of the path of this one. Neither one of them had.

"I asked Tessa to find out. She's a reporter, so she has sources. You said yourself it was big and horrible, and you weren't telling me, so I went to her…"

He turned around at that. "Oh, so it's okay for *you* to go have your friend hunt down my information but it's not okay for me to do the same thing?"

"I was scared," she shot back, hating how her voice pitched up.

"I was worried about Zack," he countered, then looked at her. "Why on earth were you scared? What have I done to ever make you think I was any kind of threat to you and Zack?"

"You were getting too close!" Molly shouted, regretting the admission instantly. Now it was out. Who was she kidding that he hadn't felt what was growing between them? It was so huge and strong, how could he not have felt it? "Zack is so fragile," she backpedaled. "I couldn't take the chance that you'd hurt him."

"Him?" Sawyer was challenging her to admit this wasn't just about Zack.

Molly thought about saying, "Yes, him," but it seemed useless. Sawyer would see through it.

Even though she'd told herself she wasn't going to ask him, Molly heard her own voice ask, "Will you tell me what happened?" She sat down at the simple wooden chair that stood against the old Formica table. It and a sad, threadbare recliner were the only pieces of furniture in the room.

"You already know."

"I want to hear it from you."

There was a second chair at the table, but Sawyer stood, his back to the wall next to the window. Molly found his stance fitting—his back up against a wall, his body staying out of the light. She watched the pain come over him as he reached back for the memory.

"I was a cop." There was a world of disappointment behind those words. Tessa had told her he'd been suspended, which meant he technically still was a cop, but she found his use of the past tense telling. She kept silent, letting him unfurl the tragic story at his own speed despite a dozen urgent questions.

"There was a guy. A nasty piece of work, gang leader, multiple arrests, that sort of thing. I'd been after him for weeks. My partner and I caught him breaking and entering. Long story short, my partner ended up still at the scene while I went after the guy in the squad car."

Sawyer paused for a moment, drawing one hand across his eyes and taking a long breath. "High-speed pursuits are supposed to be a last resort. Especially in a city. Too much possibility for damage. But I knew this guy. I'd watched him. If he got away now, he'd disappear for months. So when he sped up, I followed. I really thought I could nail him, once and for all."

Regret washed over his features, and the headline Tessa had shown her flashed in front of Molly's eyes. High-Speed Pursuit Kills Family.

"I made the call," he said. "I chose to pursue. He was blazing through neighborhoods, and I thought if he turned onto the highway, I could get enough backup to head him off."

Molly recalled the photo. A police car smashed into a minivan smashed into the corner of a building. A ghastly, mangled image of three cars, splintered glass and tumbling bricks, with police and paramedics everywhere. Sawyer's hand unconsciously went to the upper part of his left arm, where a savage scar led down from his T-shirt sleeve.

"I made a choice," Sawyer went on. His voice was cold and monotonous, as if remembering something years before instead of the year she knew it to be. "I could have let him go, but I couldn't take the chance. I pursued. He kept speeding up, but I kept with him, shouting into the radio to get units in place to head him off. I wasn't going to let him shake me off, not like he had all the other times. I made that call."

Sawyer stopped, swallowed hard. He was looking far away, somewhere over her shoulder, somewhere not even in this room. His jaw tightened. "He barely made the corner. Skidded wildly. Nearly missed this minivan. She swerved and I swerved and..." He didn't finish.

A long, dark silence hung in the room. "A mom, two kids." His words were barely above a whisper.

The press had not been kind. Tessa had needed to do a fair bit of digging to find his name, so somehow the force had managed to keep his identity out of the stories. There was a particularly wrenching bit of television footage outside the funeral where the woman's sister was crying. Sobbing, "Murder, that's what it was, murder," as she clutched a family photo of a happy mother and two smiling boys.

The gang member Sawyer had been chasing was charged with felony murder since his actions caused the deaths, but no one seemed to care about that. The stories all declared, Cop Makes Wrong Call. Sawyer was right about him being hated.

When his gaze finally returned to her, it was empty. Cold. "You asked me if it was terrible. It was. It is. And now I'm the monster again. It was dumb to think I could outrun it, even for a little while."

Molly had always been grateful for how the city's ugly news rarely made it up the mountain into Wander Canyon. Was that a blessing or a curse right now? Would she have ever asked Sawyer to teach Zack had she known?

She stared at him, struggling to connect the vilified Denver policeman with the wounded loner coffee customer she'd known. It explained so much, but there was so much dissonance there. No wonder the music had been strangled out of him. The life had been strangled out of him. Well, not entirely. She realized the desperation she'd picked up on from him was a last-chance struggle to stay human. To not be the monster too many made him out to be.

"The police investigation exonerated you."

"And you think that matters?" His voice was bitter.

Sawyer felt the last pieces of himself empty out. Was Molly really optimistic—or foolish—enough to think that his exoneration mattered? That some set of lines in the Denver Police Pursuit Policy made any difference when three innocent lives had been lost?

A hundred pages of police internal affairs reports couldn't bring that mother and her sons back. It didn't ease the grief of their family, didn't erase the images he carried. It may have validated his choice—and even then, only to some people and certainly not to him—but it hadn't changed the consequences.

Molly rose from the chair to stand straight and defiant. "You should have told me when I asked. And you should never have gone to Steve."

She was hurt. And angry. Rightfully so, and on his account. Once again his good intentions had met with terrible results. "I should have done a lot of things."

It used to be that the light and hope he saw in Molly's eyes made him feel like just maybe things might work out someday. He had let that light seep into him. He'd let it warm him just enough to make him believe he might someday escape his gloom. He'd let himself care for Zack and try to give the kid a way out of his anxieties. To let Zack feel like he'd be okay someday, maybe even someday soon. And he'd attempted one brave—okay, maybe stupid—act to give Zack the thing he most needed. And what had it done? It had just made everything worse. Everything he had done had made things worse.

Now the total lack of light and hope he saw in Molly's eyes confirmed what he'd known all along—some people didn't get light and hope. Some people were destined for lousy. His biggest mistake was letting Molly start to convince him otherwise. To let himself care.

He was totally empty now, just a shell of something that used to be him. He realized, with the last shred of feeling he had left, that he was also heartbroken. That was so sad he almost laughed. How cruel was it to discover you still had a heart by realizing it had been crushed to pieces?

"I can be gone by the weekend. Maybe sooner." Honestly, Sawyer couldn't really think of anything stopping him from walking away right now.

She glared at him. "What?"

"Leaving. I can be gone. That's what you want, isn't it? Me and my trail of disaster far away from you and Zack?"

Molly planted her hands on her hips. "You think that's the answer here? Just walking away from the mess because it's messy? Yanking yourself out of Zack's life? Don't you think he's had enough of that already?"

He couldn't stay. He'd always known he couldn't stay.

She took a step toward him, and Sawyer felt his back flatten up against the wall. "Will you give me the courtesy of an honest answer if I ask you something?"

The woman had a talent for asking impossible questions. Sawyer looked at the floor, stuffed his hands in his pockets and mumbled, "I'll try."

She held her silence until he looked back up at her. Molly was invasive—there wasn't another word for her. She wouldn't stay distant or polite or casual or uninvolved. She'd forced herself into his life, almost against his will. If he allowed himself to think about how grateful he was for that, for even a moment, his heart would break all the way into nothing. Maybe it had already.

"Do you *want* to leave?"

That wasn't a fair question. "I have to."

"That's not what I asked. Tell me the honest, messy truth, Sawyer. Do you want to leave?"

It felt like cracking his chest open to say, "No." Even the pain he felt here, deep as it was, wouldn't be as bad as the nothingness he'd feel if he went anywhere else.

"Then don't." She just stood there, as if it were that easy.

"It's not that simple."

"I think it is. Oh, it's not easy. It's hard. Really hard. Leaving's easy, but it's way worse. I'm furious at you. I'm frustrated. I'm not at all sure how we get it into that thick head of yours what it means to be part of a community."

"I'm not part of this community," he balked, her touchy-feely words ridiculous to him. Just as ridiculous was her belief that he had somehow gotten connected here. Just the opposite—he'd gone to great lengths to stay disconnected.

"You are," she countered. "I...we..." She threw her hands up in frustration. "You are."

He suddenly realized he needed to know. "Do you want me to leave?" He wasn't even asking about Zack. He was asking about her. She'd know that.

Her eyes narrowed. "I'm so mad at you right now I could spit. And I don't get mad at people very often."

Molly lived life at one hundred and ten percent. That was what drew him so strongly to her. He hadn't lived even half a life since the accident. She had all this passion for life and people, and it had felt good to let himself get sucked into just the edges of it. Somewhere down inside his empty self he found the guts to say, "That's not what I asked."

Molly crossed her arms over her chest. "What else haven't you told me?"

He knew it right then. If he chose to stay, he had to stay on Molly's terms. Honesty. Trying at this community thing. Sticking around for Zack. Dana's earlier words came back to him, the ones about being the solution Steve wouldn't be. He'd always hated it when Dana was right.

It should be a hard decision. After all, he'd made the opposite choice for months now. But the truth was staring him in the face—literally. Molly knew now. She'd seen the worst of him and still didn't want him to leave. The persistence in that woke something up inside him. That whole mercy business she talked about—maybe this was what it looked like. He didn't deserve it, and she was offering it anyway. Wasn't that how she said it worked?

He felt exposed. Indebted. Out of control. Lousy. It was way more uncomfortable than he'd guessed. Now his own words came back to him. *Not lousy, just new.*

What would he show to Zack if he left now because it got messy? Maybe he really was ready to do the work it would take to stay. It'd be worth it. Zack was worth it. Molly was worth it.

She simply stood there, expecting an answer.

The biggest surprise was that there really wasn't another big secret. He'd taken one incident and let it define his entire life. Why hadn't he seen that until just this moment?

Molly. Molly was why. Molly was the answer to a lot of whys.

A small spark of returning life accompanied his answer to her demand for further secrets: "I hate the Beatles."

Molly shook her head in confusion. "What?"

"The Beatles. Everybody thinks they're the best band in the world and I know you love their music and the whole world disagrees with me, but I can't stand them."

Something wondrous lit behind her eyes. "That's a terrible opinion."

"I know. And you'll probably hold it against me."

"I may have to." Just enough of the old Molly returned to let him exhale.

They'd come back from the edge. Molly had pushed him up to the brink of the big dark abyss that could easily swallow him, but they had turned back. He hadn't thought that possible. He'd always dug his heels in against his slow drag to the edge of the cliff, sure once he got to it there was no hope but to jump over.

But there wasn't "no hope," there was hope. It just took work. It took Molly.

She was still looking at him like he was a circus freak. "Seriously. You hate the Beatles. *No one* hates the Beatles." Her scowl was the most adorable thing he'd ever seen. He knew, right at that moment, that he would do whatever it took not to leave.

"No one but me, evidently." It took him a minute to recognize the sensation that showed up. Relief. A messy, hard-won tendril of relief pushed up inside Sawyer. The weight that had pushed against him nonstop since the accident lifted just the littlest bit. It wasn't all gone—maybe it would never be all gone—but it had lifted a little. Even if staying meant he was only allowed on the edges of her life and Zack's, it would be worth the effort it would take. Relief was here, not in hiding somewhere else. Not in hiding at all.

"You have a lot of changing to do." Her voice was tender but serious. They weren't talking about music anymore.

"I know." With a pop of clarity, it hit him what he had to do next. "I'm sorry. I should have trusted you enough to tell you about the accident. And I shouldn't have gone to Steve without telling you."

"You shouldn't have gone to Steve at all."

He wasn't quite ready to concede that. "That man needed to hear what he was throwing away."

Sawyer could see the sentiment behind that statement sink into Molly. He wasn't ready to tell her how much he cared about her, but that would come close enough for now.

"Apology accepted."

They both glanced at each other and around the dim room, unsure what to do next.

It gave him an idea. "Come play golf on Friday. I'll find a set of clubs for you."

She waved him away. "No, that's Zack's thing."

"It doesn't have to be." Sawyer cringed at his insistence, feeling as awkward as a teenager asking a way-out-of-his-league girl out on a date.

"It should be." There was something off about her answer. Her tone and her eyes didn't match. He wasn't quite sure how he knew that. Maybe it was just wishful thinking on his part. She'd told him before she wanted golf to be about Zack and nothing more. Who was he to try and push back on that? Just because they'd made peace as friends didn't mean the door had been opened for anything more than friendship.

Only Sawyer knew—now more than ever—that what he wanted didn't stop at friendship.

# Chapter Seventeen

Sawyer stood beside the Mountain Vista parking lot Friday morning with a bakery box in his hand. *This was a dumb idea. Carrot cake. Not exactly the path to a woman's heart, is it?* But since Zack had let it slip it was Molly's favorite, he'd somehow thought it was a good idea to meet her with a slice as she dropped Zack off for today's lesson.

He knew the minute she pulled up it was going to be a rough day. Molly's eyes looked tired and strained, and Zack's chin was practically sunk into his chest. The boy scrambled out of the back seat and yanked his little bag of clubs onto the grass as Molly closed her eyes, hanging on to the last shreds of her composure.

"Maybe it was a good day for this after all," he said, handing her the box through the front passenger window she'd lowered.

She raised an eyebrow in surprise.

"Carrot cake," he offered. "Zack said it was your favorite."

Sawyer wasn't sure what to make of the fact that his

gift welled up tears in her eyes. He'd done something wrong. "I just figured I owed you," he explained. The "I wanted to do something nice for you" he'd planned to say no longer seemed to fit the moment.

"Thank you," she said, her voice thin and unsteady. "It is my favorite. But you don't owe me."

*I do. A lot*, Sawyer thought but didn't say. He did manage a quiet "You okay?" as Zack stomped off toward the putting greens.

"Fine," she managed, looking anything but.

"I'll go catch up with Zack. Go find someplace peaceful and enjoy that cake. I'll see how much of the grump I can get out of him before you come back." On an impulse he added, "How about I bring him back for you? I can drop him off at home and give you a bit more time?"

"You'd do that?" She looked way more grateful than an extra twenty minutes of solitude should warrant, but maybe that was the world some days to a single mother.

"Sure." He gestured toward the back seat. "I'll need that booster seat thing, right?"

"Oh, um…yeah, you will."

He caught her reflection in the rearview mirror as he unstrapped the booster seat. She was barely holding it together. Something was wrong, something more than just a bad day from Zack. *Keep an eye on her.* He flung the thought heavenward before he realized that just might be considered a prayer.

Zack was a touchy, sour mess for most of the lesson. Foul moods usually made for terrible golf, and today was no exception. Sawyer was just about to call off any hope of learning when he realized Zack was crying.

Crying? He had no idea how to deal with little boys in tears. Anger and fear he recognized, but crying?

He walked over to Zack. "Whoa. Hey, what's wrong?" He tried to give his voice the soft tones Molly always used.

"You gave Mom cake. Did you give Mom cake because she's sick? People always brought Mom cake when she was sick." A gush of fearful words tumbled out of the poor guy. "She's sick again, isn't she? I heard her talking about doctors to someone when she thought I was in bed." His lower lip trembled and the full onslaught of tears came. "Mom's gonna die, isn't she?"

"Whoa. Slow down there, Zack." He came up close to Zack, who simply wrapped his arms around Sawyer's legs and sobbed. Sawyer sank to the grass and pulled the boy onto his lap. "Hey. Hang on there." He held the boy's heaving shoulders and tried to think of comforting things to say. "It's okay," he said over and over as he patted Zack on the back. He was terrible at this sort of thing.

Finally, as Zack seemed to get all the chaos out and catch his breath, Sawyer leaned back to catch the boy's red-rimmed gaze. "Where'd all that come from?"

"Mom was really sick when I was l-l-little," Zack offered in a damp stutter.

*You're still little*, Sawyer thought with a surge of affection that stole his breath. "I know that," he said as he fished a tissue from his pocket and held it out. "But she's okay now." After he said that, Sawyer realized he didn't actually know that to be true. He'd assumed all her distress to be on account of his going to Steve, but maybe there was more. It seemed beyond wrong, beyond all that mercy she always talked about, if she really was sick again. A wail of a *No!* to match Zack's tears welled up in Sawyer's gut.

"She's not okay," Zack replied, ignoring the offered tissue and wiping his nose on his sleeve. "She won't tell me, but she's not. She's sad a lot and Miss Tessa gives her funny looks when she thinks I can't see." He looked up at Sawyer with desperate eyes. "Is she really sick again? Is she gonna die?"

What was he supposed to say to that? It seemed beyond cruel not to deny it, but Sawyer had no idea. In fact, he'd gotten the same sense that Molly was hiding something. Something big enough to put a major dent in that nonstop optimism of hers.

He decided to take it apart, piece by piece. "Let's slow down here a minute. No sense getting all worked up just yet. Deep breaths, just like I taught you before you hit the ball." Sawyer modeled the steadying breath and watched Zack follow suit.

"Better?"

Zack sniffled and gave a damp nod.

"For starters, I gave your mom cake because it's her favorite—you told me that. And I just wanted to do something nice for her, that's all."

"'Cuz you like her." Zack said it as if it were that simple.

Sawyer debated denying it, but instead said, "I think your mom's a pretty special person."

"She likes you."

Sawyer pulled back. "How do you figure that?"

"I heard her talking to Miss Tessa. She's scared to like you, but she does. You sorta seem scared, too. I don't get how that works."

*Me neither, kid.* "Grown-up stuff can be scary sometimes. But let's talk about your mom. Does she look sick to you? Act sick? Because she seems pretty fine to me."

"Well, no."

Sawyer searched for other evidence a seven-year-old would understand. "Is she in the hospital? Going to lots of doctors?"

"No. But she could be going while I'm at camp." This kid had a real talent for finding the negative in things.

"Maybe, maybe not." He tried to keep his tone of voice respectful and patient, the way he'd seen Molly talk Zack through one of his episodes. "Have you asked her if she's sick?"

"She won't tell me."

"Your mom doesn't seem like the kind of person to lie to you. It's better than making scary stuff up that may not be true at all." A solution came to him. "Do you want me to ask her? I mean, since you seem to think we like each other and all, I'd be okay with that." He'd just admitted his complex feelings to a second grader. This, from the guy who never admitted any feelings to anyone.

"Can you do that?" Zack was probably right to be skeptical. He was a bit skeptical himself.

"I'll try." And then, it was as if some other, much nobler man added, "Friends do stuff like that for each other."

The change in Zack's face just about broke Sawyer's heart open. "We're friends, aren't we?"

Sawyer fought off the giant lump in his throat. "Yep."

"Can we play some music before we go home?"

Sawyer eased himself up off the ground. For the second time in three days he felt as if he'd backed away from a steep cliff. "Sure thing. Any song you want."

Zack's smile was worth a million dollars. "'Frog Legs.'"

Picking up Zack's golf bag, Sawyer kept his arm around the boy's shoulders. "'Frog Legs' it is."

Molly stared out her front window, looking for the lights of Sawyer's truck coming down the street. She couldn't imagine what had happened when Sawyer said he was bringing Zack back later after stopping for hot dogs. Maybe he was being kind to her, giving her extra time to wrestle her composure back from the stress of the day. The tests from Dr. Swanson's office were delayed. That wasn't a good thing. She was sure that negative results came back quickly and positives took longer.

*I'm so scared, Lord. For me and for Zack. I haven't got it in me to go through this again.*

Just when she was starting to call Sawyer's cell phone, she saw lights come up the street and turn into her drive. It took a heap of self-control not to bolt out the front door in maternal panic.

Instead, she opened the door and attempted a cheery wave—until Sawyer reached into the back seat and hoisted a sleeping Zack onto his broad shoulders.

The image cut her to the core. Sawyer held Zack with such care. His face held such a "Did I do this right?"

expression that she nearly laughed. She held the door open so he could angle himself through—a maneuver that brought him unsettlingly close to her—and she pointed up the stairs toward Zack's room.

"How'd you tire him out like that?" she asked when Sawyer came back down the stairs. "He can never sleep when he gets all worked up like he was." She felt she had to add, "Sorry to dump him on you in one of his moods, but we were on our last nerves with each other today."

"So I noticed," he replied.

Molly motioned toward the kitchen. "The least I could do is offer you a coffee. But there's no carrot cake left. I gobbled up both slices on the way home from the golf course."

Sawyer seemed amused, rather than judgmental. She liked that. "Did it help?"

"Carrot cake always helps. I've found cake in general to be a pretty handy coping strategy." She felt a small glow start up in her stomach as she added, "Thank you."

Sawyer stood across from her in the small kitchen. He seemed to fill the room, making her extra aware of his presence even though he'd been in the house several times before.

He leaned against the counter as she put the hot water on and got out a bag of Colombian decaf grounds. "I made a promise to a friend," he said, "so I have to ask you something."

That was a weird way to put it. She turned away from him toward her cabinets to fetch the French press coffeepot. "Okay, shoot."

He lowered his voice, and she sensed him taking a

step closer to her. "Are you sick again, Molly? Is the cancer back?"

She nearly dropped the glass carafe. A vulnerable panic raced down her spine and squeezed her breath tight. She couldn't pull in enough air to answer.

"Zack thinks you are, and he's scared out of his wits. He poured it all out to me today, poor guy."

Molly was already crying by the time she turned to look at him.

His eyes were full of pain and alarm. "You are, aren't you?"

"I don't know." It came out in a whispered wail. "Maybe. I found…something. They're running tests. They should be back by now and they're not and I'm sure that means it's bad news and…"

His arms were around her in an instant. She found herself melting against him as Zack had done in his sleep. Sawyer was silent and solid and steady against her, a fortress against the tears she could no longer hold at bay. Every mother knows how to cry without anyone hearing, but it suddenly became okay, maybe even good, that Sawyer was there to hear. The tears erupted out of her with a surprising force, and she let them come.

"Shhh," he said, keeping a tight grip even when she tried to pull back. "Shhh." His voice held a tenderness she'd never heard from him.

After a minute or so, worry over Zack pulled her from the sadness. "He knows?" That broke her heart. She'd tried so hard to keep any hint of her worry from him. Some days Zack's acute powers of observation were a curse.

Sawyer brushed a strand of hair from over her eye,

and she felt the care of the gesture deep into her bones. He did not move to step away from her, and she could not bring herself to step away from him. "He suspects. He overheard you talking to Tessa, and he thinks people bringing you cake means you're sick."

Molly shook her head. That was pure Zack, imagining alarming connections between events that weren't connected at all. "I'm sorry you got caught up in all this."

"I'm not." He meant it. It glowed like a promise in his eyes. "I mean, it's not my strong suit, but I was glad to be the person he could unload on. We get each other, Zack and I."

Sawyer seemed to consider that a weird accident. She knew better. "Do you realize what a gift that is? To him?" Despite her resistance, she couldn't help but add, "To me?"

Now it was he who shook his head. "I'm no gift to anybody."

The world had beaten so much of his self-worth out of him. "You're wrong. You're scarred, but most of us are." She reached her hand up and ran it across the strong angle of his jaw. He sucked in a breath, stunned by the touch.

"Molly..." It was more of a breath than a word. Did he realize what it did to her when he said her name like that?

His tortured tone and the longing in his eyes tore down the last of her defenses. Giving in to the flood of care and tenderness that overtook her, Molly leaned in and kissed him. A soft, sweet kiss, a careful, shaky thing that dared to cross all the space between them. He held still, as if worried the slightest movement would scare her away. But when she slid her arms around his neck, his whole body responded as if she'd handed him the secret of life. Maybe she had.

One hand held her tight while the other cupped her face tenderly. She could feel the surprise and wonder in his racing pulse, in the breaths that matched her own. What an extraordinary thing it was to be so surprised by something you knew all along. The small pull she'd felt from that first morning in the coffee shop bloomed into something full and rich and worth every struggle.

When the sheer power of the moment felt as if it was getting beyond them, Molly pulled back to catch her breath. "Wouldn't it shock Zack to walk in on that?" She rolled her eyes. Probably not the best response to an epic kiss like that.

Sawyer's laugh was rich and low. "Actually, no. He knows."

Molly stared at him. "He what?"

"He figured it out. Today he told me I like you and you like me. Simple as that." Sawyer slid his hand down her arm to grasp her hand. It was a simple, affectionate gesture, but to Molly it held as much power as the breathtaking kiss. He smirked. "He also told me neither of us wants to admit it. Smart kid."

Molly felt her cheeks redden. "I think we just did a pretty good job of admitting it."

"I suppose so."

"How long?" Had it been steadily growing for him, as well?

She would have never in a million years thought that Sawyer's eyes could sparkle. It was as if the layers of darkness were sliding off him right in front of her eyes. "You've been the best part of my day. That impossible cheer you carry around. I can never get enough of it."

Even feeling that way, he'd gone to Steve to try to restore her family. What she'd thought was arrogance was actually an act of service, of sacrifice. She felt a new tear slip down her cheek. They'd muddled so much of this, and yet God had still led them here.

"So it wasn't just my great coffee after all?" she teased.

He smiled. "That, too. But when I began to realize just how much you were dealing with, and still…well, I don't know how you keep that cheer."

She gave him a look. "Yeah, you do. I've already told you. And it's not cheer. Cheer is something that comes and goes. It's joy." She laid her hand on his heart. "Joy is something God gives us."

"Does everything always come back to God's gifts for you?" His words were teasing, but she loved the affection in his eyes.

She tapped his heart, feeling her own glow in her chest. "Uh-huh. Even you." Molly shouldn't have been so startled by how much she meant it. "You've been so far from joy for so long." She raised her hand to touch his face. "Come on back to it. Let us walk you back to it. It's closer than you think."

Sawyer's response was to close the distance between them and kiss her. This kiss was deeper, as filled with promise and hope as a kiss between two scarred people could be. The power of it showed her all the loneliness she'd endured, how solitary her heart had been.

The kiss was a pledge that she wouldn't bear whatever burdens were coming all on her own.

"What do you want to tell Zack?" he asked when they finally broke the embrace. Molly was amused at the breathless tone of his voice. The man knew how to make a woman swoon in her own kitchen.

"That he was right and I do like you and you like me," she replied.

"I meant about you. I promised him I would ask you, so I'll need to give an answer. I don't want to lie to him, but I'm worried the truth is a bit much for him. Still, it's your call. He's my friend, but he's your son. I'll do whatever you want."

Sawyer was already so much more to Zack than Steve had ever been. Molly leaned against the counter, pondering the difficult issue. "I think," she began, "I tell the truth I have for now. I'm not sick. Because I'm not. Except for being panicked with worry, I feel fine. And while I'm scared to death I might be getting sick, I'm not. Not now, at least." After a moment, she added, "Thank you. For being there for him."

"I want to be there for you, too. I'm not sure how, and I'll probably mess it up in a million ways, but I want you to know. I'm ready to stay." His voice broke a bit on that declaration, and Molly marveled at what it meant for him to say that. "Even when it gets messy," he went on. "Some wacky, *joyful* lady told me that was important."

She loved that he used the word *joy*. How incredible that her heart was so full of wonder and hope when it had been crushed in fears mere hours ago. "'Bridge Over Troubled Water,'" she said, recalling that wondrous time in the church sanctuary. So many of the lyrics fit the moment, Molly was sure it was no accident it had been the first song they'd shared together.

"Yeah, that," he said. "Maybe we can learn a few more."

"I'd like that." At this moment, nothing meant more to her in the world.

# Chapter Eighteen

Two days later, Sawyer found himself in church. Willingly. If that didn't showcase the power of God Almighty, Sawyer wasn't sure what would. *Well*, he thought to himself as he sat in a pew—a *front* pew—with Molly and Zack, *God and the mighty powers of Molly Kane's relentless persuasion.*

On the outside, nothing had really changed. He still had a dead-end night job on the outskirts of town. He still didn't know what—or if—he'd ever be in law enforcement ever again. Zack was still an anxious little guy for whom life was a daily struggle. Molly still didn't have test results, so, while she was doing her best to hide it, she was as full of anxieties as her son.

It was the inside that had changed. Words like *grace* and *hope* had been fluffy, nonexistent ideas in his life for years. Even before the accident, if he was honest. Life had felt like a long battle he was losing by degrees.

That was changing. Right before his eyes, it seemed. Little bits at a time, but in tiny ways that made a huge difference.

"And now we'll be blessed by our choir," announced Pastor Newton. "And I want to take this moment to thank Sawyer Bradshaw for filling in while Samantha's arm heals. Most of you don't know Sawyer, but I trust you'll show him a warm welcome after the service."

Molly smiled. A broad, "you're one of us whether you like it or not now" smile he felt warm his chest like the clear sunshine beaming in through the tall church windows. He took the look she gave him as she stepped apart from the choir to sing her solo and tucked it in a corner of his heart. Having Molly make him coffee had always been the highlight of his day. Hearing Molly sing was becoming his oxygen, his sunlight and his doorway back into the world.

He waited for her nod, then began the opening chords. Playing the piano while Molly sang felt like home—the place he'd been heading for this whole time without knowing it. The song spoke to him of faith and journey, of imperfection and grace. Molly's faith sailed out into the sanctuary on her gorgeous voice. He yearned for what she had, and this morning, for the first time, Sawyer began to believe it was possible. If faith really was the gift she described, then he could ask for it. He could receive it. He could rebuild his life on it.

The rest of the choir came in on the chorus, and the sound built to soar around the space. It wasn't perfect—far from—but it was heartfelt. This was what people meant by worship. This was why two-hundred-year-old hymns still meant something today.

When he thought the moment couldn't get more powerful, Pastor Newton lifted his hands and the whole congregation joined in. A swell of voices—some lovely, some gravelly, some loud, some soft—built upon the choir's notes. For a split second Sawyer looked over and saw Zack singing at the top of his voice. He was getting most of the words wrong, but the boy's enthusiasm pulled down the last of Sawyer's resistance.

He joined in. Humming at first, and then startling himself by singing. Terribly, probably, but why had he never realized that didn't matter? The powerful words sank into him as he sang, holy and healing.

Molly looked over the moment she realized he had added his voice, her eyes full of joy. And maybe a tear or two. For that matter, Sawyer felt his own voice thicken up with the power of the moment. His fingers wove prayers over the keyboard, his voice—all their voices—sent prayers into his heart.

*Thank You.* Sawyer sent the prayer silently up into the rafters to join the echo of the voices as the song ended. He could not remember the last time he felt this useful, this purposeful, this okay with his place in the world. *Thank You.* There was a lot God still needed to set right in his life and the world around him, but thanks were more than enough for now.

"You can't sing any better than I can," Zack whispered as they took their place in the pew after the hymn.

"I'm glad that doesn't matter," Sawyer said. When had he become the kind of man who could say something like that? "Your mom makes up for the both of us."

Sawyer sat back and let the rest of the service pour over him. And afterward, it wasn't so hard to stand around the cozy little church parlor sipping good coffee from paper cups and accepting compliments from churchgoers.

"Look at you!" Chaz Walker said as he balanced a coffee in one hand and Henry, his squirmy toddler, on the opposite hip. "I always say you can only hide from WCCC for so long."

"I tried," Sawyer confessed.

"Me, too," Chaz said in a tone that hinted there was a long story behind that admission.

"There's a bunch of us who could make that claim," Wyatt Walker said as he joined them. He made a face at Henry. "There's no hope for you, little guy. They got you in here already, so you're a goner from the start."

Sawyer didn't feel like a goner at all. He felt like someone who had finally come to his senses.

"So," Wyatt said with a wry smile. "Molly." The two words held a dozen implications.

He'd been sitting with Molly in church. He'd kissed her in her own kitchen. Rather soundly. He'd always had an attraction to her, but now he knew he'd truly fallen for her. "Um…yeah," he admitted, running one hand nervously through his hair. Was that okay to admit publicly? He felt as if his entire being broadcast it in neon colors—Molly's, too.

Chaz laid a hand on his shoulder. "I'm happy for you, man. Wander Canyon women are one of a kind."

"Hey," Wyatt teased his brother, "you imported yours." Sawyer had heard the story from Molly about how Chaz had brought Yvonne from North Carolina when Chaz's stepfather married Yvonne's aunt. This town seemed to specialize in unusual—and dramatic—

romances. Were he and Molly on their way to being another of them?

With a shocked but happy surprise, Sawyer realized that he wouldn't mind that at all.

"Molly's pretty amazing," Wyatt commented. "Great barista and that golden voice. A man could do a lot worse."

"Yeah," Sawyer agreed. Maybe small talk with neighbors wasn't so hard after all. "And Zack. He's a special little guy, you know?"

"I'd say the guy willing to build him an award-winning hippo cart has a lot going for him, too. And you play a mean piano. I think we'll all be willing to look past the golf resort thing…eventually."

Sawyer stiffened for a moment, until he realized Wyatt was kidding. It had never occurred to him that people would eventually look past his employer. He'd thought it guaranteed him a position as town outcast.

Of course, that was before Molly Kane.

Suddenly, as much as Sawyer liked his new friends, he wanted to be near Molly. The urge to be beside her, to be seeing her, holding her hand, talking with her, had become a near constant ache. He'd fallen hard for that woman.

Sawyer smiled at Wyatt and Chaz, but found himself looking over their shoulders to scan the room for Molly or Zack.

"Speaking of goners," Wyatt teased again. "Go find her, man. We don't blame you one bit."

"Thanks," Sawyer said, feeling weirdly exposed and yet like he was among friends for the first time in a long while. He'd been chasing solitude for so long he'd forgotten how good it felt to be connected. And he had Molly to thank.

The urge to tell her, to thank her—and maybe steal one more kiss from her—sent him from the room to hunt through the halls of the church.


Molly stood at the edge of the church lawn, pulling in a deep breath. She stared at the *Call me* text on her cell phone, willing herself to press the icon that would dial her oncologist's number.

Dr. Swanson wouldn't text on a Sunday morning for just anything. This had to be the test results. She could make the case that it was bad news just as much that it was good news. Whichever, it was clearly news Dr. Swanson felt couldn't wait.

*Oh, Father, protect me either way. I know You're with me whether it's good or bad, but I'm scared to death here.* Digging for a blessing, Molly tried to be thankful that she'd seen the message notification while Zack was occupied with friends from church. She needed to hear this news alone.

Or did she? Molly heard a noise and looked up to see Sawyer coming toward her. It was hard to believe the man had changed as much as he had since they'd admitted everything to each other. So much of his darkness was gone, and an extraordinary man was appearing. The intensity of his eyes was transforming from pain to…well, to something that could make her stomach flip with a single glance.

It was endearing how he sent a glance over his shoulder back toward the church before he took her hand.

"Hey," he said, noticing her expression. "Everything okay?"

That was the million-dollar question at the moment, wasn't it? "I think I'm about to find out." Her voice shook a bit as she held up the screen so he could see the text.

"Test results?" Sawyer's grip on her other hand tightened. Gratitude for even that tiny show of reassurance pushed back against the fear.

She could only manage a nod.

"Do you want me to go? Do you need to hear this alone?"

*No. I want you beside me when I hear this.* The depth of her response showed Molly just how used she'd become to shouldering everything alone. "Please stay."

She was about to tap the icon to dial when Sawyer stayed her hand. He stared into her eyes for a long moment, then kissed her. His touch felt filled with a promise that was both strong and tender. Without a single word, he let her know that this kiss stood solid no matter what the next moments held. He would, truly, stay even if it got messy. Tears filled her eyes at the powerful gesture.

Molly pulled in a breath as Sawyer's arms wrapped around her. It was a strange, beautiful gift to be able to put the call on speakerphone. A tiny detail confirming she wouldn't do this alone.

Molly tried not to read disaster in the fact that Dr. Swanson picked up almost immediately. "Hello, Molly."

"Hi, Doc." Her voice nearly squeaked with anxiety.

"I knew you'd be okay with a Sunday morning call. I know how much you've been waiting for these test results."

"And…" Molly shut her eyes, preparing for her world to tilt.

"Exhale, Molly. There's no indication of cancer. Just a benign mass. We can remove it if you like, but there's no need. You're cancer-free. I want you to contact me whenever you find anything that concerns you, but your cancer has not returned."

Molly felt Sawyer exhale behind her, felt his head fall to touch hers. Relief flooded through the both of them. It felt as if it flooded through the whole canyon.

"I'm so glad to hear that." She didn't bother to hide the tears in her voice. "You have no idea how glad I am to hear that."

"I knew it couldn't wait," Dr. Swanson said. "And I'm glad, too. You're fine, Molly. You're just fine."

Molly leaned back against Sawyer's chest. It felt so wonderful to have someone to lean on. "Thanks a million, Doc."

"My pleasure, Molly. I'll see you for your regular checkup in six months unless you need me for anything else. You take care, now."

Molly's hands were shaking as she ended the call. Sawyer turned her to face him, taking her face gently in his hands. He wiped her wet cheek with one thumb, eyes full of the same relief sweeping through her. "I'd be beside you no matter what," he said with the solemnity of a promise. "But I'm so glad you're okay. Thank God."

How wondrous to know he truly meant those last two words. Molly always considered it a privilege to watch someone's faith unfold, but how amazing to watch it in the man she had come to love.

She leaned into the touch of his palm against her

cheek. "I love you." There had been a time when she wondered if she would ever say those words again. The surprise of saying them to Sawyer seemed nothing less than a gift from Heaven.

His eyes took on a gleam she'd never seen in Sawyer. "Hey, I wanted to be the one to say it first."

Molly's whole soul seemed to lighten with her laughter. "Beat you to it, I guess."

His grin faded into a serious look. "I'm so grateful you pushed yourself into my life. I love Zack. I love you." He kissed her again, and then nodded back toward the church. "And they've figured it out."

Molly laughed, deeply this time. "Wander's always watching. But I don't think anyone would have to look hard. I think it was seeping out of my pores when I sang this morning."

"Have I told you how much I love your voice? It's… there's so much light in it. I don't just hear it—" he put one hand to his chest "—I feel it." He gifted her with the warmest of smiles. "I hear you even when I'm not with you."

Molly settled her arms around his shoulders, perfectly happy to stay close to him even if all of Wander happened to be watching. "You know, I think Zack feels the same way about your music. He had me download nearly every ragtime song we could find onto his music player. I hear him humming the tunes. So I guess I hear you even when I'm not with you, too."

"How do we tell him?" The nervousness in Sawyer's eyes told her how big a step this was for him.

Her heart glowed at his courage on her behalf. "Zack? I think he already knows. You said so yourself."

Sawyer pulled her a little closer. "I think this is a little more serious than 'you like her and she likes you.'"

"Zack's a smart kid. I expect he's already figured that out, too." A sudden thought struck her. "Hey, I'm not going to have to take up golf or anything, am I?"

"Only if you want to. I'm fine with it just being Zack's and my thing. But if you got it into your mind to invite me to that choir breakfast of yours, I think I'm ready to take that up."

Sawyer? At the choir breakfast? God had truly exceeded every expectation in bringing Sawyer into this community. Molly was near dizzy with gratitude, relief… and love. Sawyer was here, holding her, making promises, making friends. "You should definitely join us for breakfast this week." She leaned in. "You should join us for a lot of things."

"I plan to. Let's go find Zack and your friends and tell them the happy news."

"The test results?"

"That, too."

Molly took his hand and together they started walking back toward the church. "What do you say we walk over to the bakery and buy the biggest carrot cake they have. I'm in the mood to celebrate, and I want Zack to know cake means good things."

Sawyer laughed. It was the first full, rich, happy laugh she'd heard from him. And she knew it would not be the last.

# *Chapter Nineteen*

"Who knew I was such a fan of waffles?" Sawyer patted his stomach after a morning breakfast with the folks from the choir. He could be exhausted from a bad shift at the resort and still make sure he made this weekly meal with friends.

Friends. He had friends—many of them—here in Wander Canyon. Almost every day it amazed him how he'd come here to hide and God worked it out so that instead he found himself. And love.

The August sun was just starting to heat up the day as he motioned to one of the benches that lined the town's main street. "Can you spare another few moments?" he asked Molly, knowing she was on her break from the coffee shop. "I've got something I want to show you."

"For you? Absolutely."

They sat down and Sawyer pulled a letter from his pocket. It had taken him four days to write it, and his trash can at the apartment was filled with crumpled versions. Still, he'd known this was something he had to do, and something he wanted to share with her.

"This is to the surviving family of the mom and boys killed in the accident. It's telling them how sorry I am and asking for their forgiveness."

She touched the envelope with reverence. She knew what a monumental thing it was. "Oh, Sawyer."

"I'd always thought the ruling by Internal Affairs would clear my conscience, but it never did. I need to do this. Thank you for showing me that."

She looked up at him. "I didn't show you that, God did."

"Well, I'm not sure He would have gotten through without your help."

"Do you think they'll respond?" she asked. "They said some pretty awful things."

Sawyer sighed and sat back against the bench. "I'm not sure it matters if they do. This was a step I needed to take. To make peace with what happened. To be able to move forward." It stunned him again how easily a smile came to him when he looked at her. "I'm cooking up some big plans."

Her eyes widened. He loved surprising her. "Really?"

He'd almost announced this at breakfast, but decided he owed a private reveal to Molly first. "Did you know there will be an opening in the Wander Canyon Police Department later his year?"

Her eyes widened even more. Followed by that glowing smile he'd come to cherish. "No, I didn't."

"I'm going to apply for a lateral transfer. There's a bunch of procedures and paperwork that needs to happen, and it's no done deal, but I'm ready. I have an appointment with Chief Perkins to talk it over next week."

She threw her arms around him. "Sawyer, that's wonderful. Day shifts?"

"I can't say for sure, but eventually, I hope." It had been a feat of coordination to spend so much time together with him still on night shifts. Sawyer no longer needed the isolation of the solitary nights. He was ready to step into the daylight in more ways than one.

"I can be patient."

He grinned. "Molly Kane, you're the least patient person I know."

He'd never tire of her laugh. It was bright and musical and sounded like sunshine. "Well, okay, I can try." She looked at her watch. "Time to get back to brewing up goodness for Wander folks." She looked again at the envelope. "This is wonderful. Really. I'm so proud of you." *Thank You for this woman, Lord*, he prayed as he walked her to The Depot as he had after every choir breakfast morning since joining the meal on the way home from Mountain Vista.

She kissed him on the steps up to the red train car, as she had done every time. "Sleep tight."

He would. He'd slept soundly lately for the first time in years.

There probably were more elegant places for this occasion, but Sawyer couldn't think of a better one than Cuccio's Pizza. November had brought a solid chill to the air, and his weekly pizza nights with Molly and Zack were still one of the highlights of his week.

Zack and Molly already at their favorite table as he walked into the restaurant. "Hi, Officer Bradshaw!" a little girl called as he headed toward the booth.

He'd made two classroom visits to Zack's school since joining the Wander Canyon police force. Third grade school visits? Some days Sawyer didn't even recognize the new person he was becoming.

He'd never been this happy.

He was pretty hopeful life was going to get even happier after tonight.

"Sorry," he said as he sat down. "I was running late and I didn't have time to change out of uniform." He leaned over and gave Molly a quick kiss. When had he become the kind of man to kiss so freely, and in public even? Love sure changed a guy.

"You'll get no grief from me," she said. "You know how much I like you in uniform."

"Mom…" Zack moaned.

"Someday you'll eat that groan," Sawyer teased.

"I'd rather eat some pizza. I'm starved." Zack clutched his stomach.

"Me, too," Sawyer admitted, "but midterm report card first. That was the deal."

Sawyer already knew the contents of the report. Molly had called him earlier this week, crying tears of joy for the compliments Zack's third grade teacher had gone out of her way to relay to Molly. Zack was thriving. Some things were still a struggle, and he had days where he slumped back into his anxieties, but it warmed Sawyer's heart to see the boy coming into his own.

Zack grinned and produced the paper. Molly, who had already seen it and called for the celebratory pizza night, beamed. "You've put in a lot of effort. And look how it's paid off. You're a terrific third grader." He made a point of catching Zack's eye. "I'm proud of you."

The resulting look on Zack's face was nothing short of a treasure. Every day Sawyer felt his affection for the boy grow.

Of course, half the excited look on Zack's face had nothing to do with the paper he held. It had a lot to do with the conversation they'd had on the golf course yesterday. To be honest, Sawyer was excited, too. Well, that and a little nervous. He was grateful for the encouragement in Zack's bright eyes.

They ordered their usual meal. They said hello to a couple of friends and neighbors eating at nearby tables or stopping in for carryout. After about ten minutes, Zack poked at Sawyer's arm before slumping back in his chair and rolling his eyes. "C'mon. You're not really going to wait all the way until after we eat, are you?"

Molly gave the pair of them one of her looks. "What is up with the two of you? You've both been fidgety the whole time. You're up to something."

Zack held up his hands. "Not me."

Sawyer pushed out a breath. He was wondering how he was going to down his usual four slices with the way his stomach was turning nervous somersaults.

Molly raised a suspicious eyebrow, making an adorably clueless face. Sawyer said a quick prayer for courage and set down his root beer.

He cleared his throat, his mind suddenly going blank of the speech he'd drafted four times last night. "I can't think of a time when I've been happier," he began, hating how his voice pitched tight with nerves. "These past seven months have been, well, amazing. Life-changing. I got my life back on account of you. You and faith and friends and all, but mostly you." He cleared his throat again, suddenly terrified.

Zack leaned over to Molly. "He wants to get married, Mom. He asked me if it was okay yesterday."

Sawyer's hand went to his forehead. "Why is everyone in this family always beating me to the punch for the important stuff?"

Molly stared at him, eyes wide in that look of wonder that could always melt him to nothing. "Because everyone in this *family*," she used the word with a heartwarming emphasis, "already loves you."

Okay, this wasn't anything close to how he'd planned this, but what in Sawyer's life these past months had gone the way he'd originally planned? Life with Molly was a nonstop adventure. Why not this, as well?

Sawyer got down on one knee in the middle of a crowded, noisy, pizza parlor and pulled a small velvet box from his pocket. He opened it to reveal the ring. "Molly Kane, will you marry me?"

Molly was in tears even before he finished the question. "Absolutely!" she said, wrapping her arms around his shoulders and kissing him.

Somewhere on the edges of his bliss, Sawyer was vaguely aware of applause coming from the crowd, punctuated by a groan of "Ugh. More kissing!" from Zack. He couldn't bring himself to care. Molly was going to be his wife. Zack would be his son. The very thought made his chest want to burst with happiness.

When Molly finally let go, he slipped the ring onto her finger and felt the whole of his life slide into place.

"Told ya she'd say yes," Zack said with astounding confidence. Sawyer had been rather nervous Zack would find such a large-scale change in his life daunting. He'd been almost as apprehensive about asking Zack as he was about asking Molly. In truth, it seemed more like Zack was wondering what took Sawyer so long.

"It's not too soon?" Sawyer whispered to Molly. He'd been worried the leap forward might test even her legendary impatience.

Her face beamed. "Officer Bradshaw, I can't marry you soon enough."

Zack suddenly pointed to the far end of the room. "Pastor Newton's right over there, you know."

Molly laughed. "That might be a bit too soon. What do you say we do a bit of planning and do it up right?"

Sawyer slipped the hand of his bride-to-be into his, marveling at the glittering diamond now gracing her fingers. A gush of gratitude flew up from his heart to God, who had surprised him with so much joy. "Make me coffee every morning for the rest of our lives?" he asked, feeling as if the smile on his face would never leave.

"I love my new family." Her eyes glistened every time she said the word. "Nothing would make me happier."

Arturo Cuccio came over to the table. "Our first proposal ever! Pizza's on the house."

"Cool," Zack said, licking his lips.

"More than cool," Molly added. "Absolutely wonderful."

Sawyer couldn't agree more.

* * * * *

Dear Reader,

I'll never be able to explain where some stories come from. They leap out of nowhere to capture your heart and demand to be told. Molly, Sawyer and precious little Zack showed up in my brain one day and begged me for their happy ending. In a world where there is so much sadness and struggle, I was glad to be able to craft their story. If their path to joy gives you hope in your own struggles, then know my prayers for these words have been fulfilled.

You'll be pleased to know more visits to Wander Canyon are in the works. Tessa gets her own happy ending in the next book—and what you discover about cranky old Norma Binton will surprise you indeed!

I always love to hear from readers. You can find me at alliepleiter.com or on Facebook, Instagram, Twitter, Pinterest, and P.O. Box 7026 Villa Park, IL 60181.

Blessings,
*Allie*

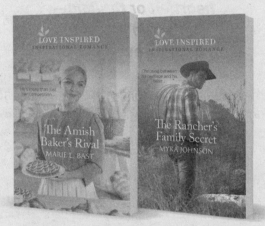

*Newly guardian to her twin nieces, Hannah Antonicelli
is determined to keep her last promise to her late
sister—that she'll never reveal the identity of their
father. But when Luke Hutchenson is hired as a
handyman at her work and begins to bond with the little
girls, hiding that he's their uncle isn't easy...*

*Read on for a sneak peek at*
Finding a Christmas Home *by Lee Tobin McClain!*

On Wednesday after work, Hannah drove toward home, the
twins in the back seat, and tried not to be nervous that Luke
was in the front seat beside her.

"I really appreciate this," he said. His car hadn't started this
morning, and he'd walked the three miles to Rescue Haven.

Of course, Hannah had insisted on driving him home. What
else could she do? It was cold outside, spitting snow, and he
was her next-door neighbor.

"I hate to ask another favor," he said, "but could you stop by
Pasquale's Pizza on the way?"

"No problem." She took a left and drove the two blocks to
the only nonchain pizza place in Bethlehem Springs.

He jumped out, and she turned back to check on the twins,
trying not to watch Luke as he headed into the shop. He was
good-looking, of course. Kind, appreciative and strong. And he
had the slightest swagger in his walk that was masculine and
appealing.

But he was also about to go visit his brother, Bobby, if he kept his promise to his ailing father. And when she'd heard about that visit, it had been a wake-up call: she shouldn't get too close with him. The fewer chances she had to spill the beans about Bobby being the twins' father, the better.

He came out of the pizza shop quickly—he must have called ahead—carrying a big flat box and a white bag. What would it be like if this was a family scenario, if they were Mom and Dad and kids, stopping for takeout on the way home from work?

She couldn't help it. Her chest filled with longing.

He climbed into her small car, juggling the large flat box to make it fit without encroaching on the gearshift.

She had to laugh at the size of his meal. "Hungry?"

"Are you?" He opened the box a little, and the rich, garlicky fragrance of Pasquale's special sauce filled the car.

Her stomach growled, loudly.

"Pee-zah!" Addie shouted from the back seat.

"Peez!" Emmy added, almost as loud.

"That's just cruel," she said as she pulled the car back onto the road and steered toward Luke's place. "You're tempting us. I may have to order some when I get these girls home."

"No, you won't," he said. "This is for all of us. The least I can do is feed you, after you drove me around."

Her stomach gave a little leap, and not just about the prospect of pizza. Why was he inviting her to have dinner with him? Was there an ulterior motive? And if there was, would she mind?

*Don't miss*
Finding a Christmas Home *by Lee Tobin McClain,*
*available October 2021 wherever*
*Love Inspired books and ebooks are sold.*

LoveInspired.com

LIEXP0921

# IF YOU ENJOYED THIS BOOK, DON'T MISS NEW EXTENDED-LENGTH NOVELS FROM LOVE INSPIRED!

**In addition to the Love Inspired books you know and love, we're excited to introduce even more uplifting stories in a longer format, with more inspiring fresh starts and page-turning thrills!**

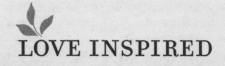

# LOVE INSPIRED

*Stories to uplift and inspire.*

Fall in love with Love Inspired—inspirational and uplifting stories of faith and hope. Find strength and comfort in the bonds of friendship and community. Revel in the warmth of possibility, and the promise of new beginnings.

**LOOK FOR THESE LOVE INSPIRED TITLES ONLINE AND IN THE BOOK DEPARTMENT OF YOUR FAVORITE RETAILER!**